CHAPTER 1

Sensei Akeni whistled as he walked down Amplebury High Street. An innocuous looking little man; pork pie hat, long grey old fashioned raincoat, he walked with the slightly bowed shoulders and the shuffle that is the sign of an experienced judoka. He was five feet five inches tall, and one of the highest judoka in the country; ninth dan.

He casually strolled into the local branch of the Eastern Bank, intending to deposit a small sum from his expenses as local delegate to the Pan World Judo Conference. He whistled as he stepped inside; a skippy pentatonic oriental-sounding tune.

Then – uproar. The gruff boom of a shotgun, screams, sound of a body falling. Then four black-clad and balaclava-ed figures ran towards him. Seizing the first by his black jacket, Sensei executed a perfect *ippon seoinaga* to throw him over his shoulder and land him on his back. The mask slipped – just a little. Akeni turned round to face the next man when a shotgun barrel was rammed into his gut followed by a blow on the head. Darkness closed in.

He came round groggily to the two-toned shrieks of emergency vehicles, and a sea of concerned faces gazing down at him. Voices didn't make any sense to him, and he found he had forgotten all his English. Slowly coming round, he began to recognise speech,

'Brave little guy, that,' came a man's voice.

'Don't you know who that is?' A young person's voice, tinged with awe and admiration, 'That's Sensei Akeni, local judo club teacher. Does a lot of work especially with schools.'

Akeni tried to bow politely, but couldn't move.

Just then he was cocooned in a bright red blanket, lifted easily into the gape of an ambulance and two-toned away.

Hours passed in a haze of concussion and morphine, until finally he recovered consciousness. He found a godlike consultant dressed in striped trousers, black jacket and a red rose in his buttonhole looming authoritatively over him, requesting details of pulse, temperature and wound from a meek acolyte nurse. Pronouncing himself satisfied, the Being enquired, 'DO-YOU-SPEAK-ENGLISH?" in the slow, staccato clear shout that every Englishman knows every foreigner understands.

'I speak perfect English,' replied Sensei, bowing his head politely, 'I learned while pursuing my degree and chosen profession of physiologist in and around Cambridge.'

'in that case,' the consultant replied at a less decibel level, 'do you feel all right to be questioned by the police?'

'Certainly.'

Inspector Forbes came gently into the room and moved the chair so the patient could see him full face. He was tall, slightly given to embonpoint, but still muscular, with a physical competence that a suit of Burton's best and a nondescript tie could not hide. He sat down quietly at the side of the bed.

'What can you tell me about the raid, Mr Akeni?' spoken very quietly and non-official.

'Not a lot, I'm afraid. As I entered the bank, I heard a shotgun bark, and screams. I heard a body falling.'

'How did you know it was a shotgun, Sir?'

'If you had lived through the immediate post War chaos in Japan, you would recognise every kind of weapon, Inspector.'

'What happened then?'

'I rendered one of the culprits semi-immobile, was about to take his balaclava off – it had slipped a bit – when I was violently poked in the stomach by a shotgun, and then rendered unconscious by a blow to the head – as you see!' smiling ruefully and pointing to his damaged head. 'But there is something I almost recognised about one of them, oh… glimpse of face? Maybe. Body posture? Maybe. I feel that I know this person. Ah, it's frustrating, but I will apply this mind of mine to the problem, and will let you know as soon as something surfaces.'

JUDOKILL

BILL WATSON

authorHOUSE®

AuthorHouse™ UK
1663 Liberty Drive
Bloomington, IN 47403 USA
www.authorhouse.co.uk
Phone: UK TFN: 0800 0148641 (Toll Free inside the UK)
UK Local: (02) 0369 56322 (+44 20 3695 6322 from outside the UK)

Published by AuthorHouse 10/27/2022

ISBN: 978-1-7283-7633-2 (sc)
ISBN: 978-1-7283-7634-9 (hc)
ISBN: 978-1-7283-7635-6 (e)

Print information available on the last page.

Inspector Forbes was a kindly man and a good copper, so knowing that nothing further could be teased out at the moment, he made his farewells, thanking the medical staff as he went.

Akeni lay back…what was it?…Then he slept.

Discharged that morning, given a bit of gentle humorous ragging by the nurses and junior doctors about thick skulls, Sensei Akeni let himself into the dojo. Young Smith was taking a ladies' self-defence class this afternoon. Sensei liked to stay *au fait* with the club. He trusted Smithy, even more than his other leaders, but there was always temptation with ladies' groups. Being close to warm female flesh can play havoc with any young guy. And a good looking, fit leader can cause female hearts to flutter. Pity there was yet no female judoka good enough to take over. But a gentle presence from the senior man would release both Smithy-san and his ladies from temptation. He took off his shoes and went to hang his coat up. Still chasing his elusive thought about the bank robber round and round in his head – but no joy.

He looked up, surprised, 'Hello! I wasn't expecting you. I thought this was Smithy-san's group.'

He was punched – massively - in the belly. He looked down. A six-inch kitchen knife stuck obscenely out of his sternum. 'Why?' he gasped.

'You know too much; you saw too much, old man.' Through his failing senses Sensei saw the man stroll out. Then darkness.

Twenty-five year old John Smith; Sunday School teacher, police constable and fifth dan judo instructor let himself in to the dojo.

Bowing in honour of the mat at the doorway, he removed his shoes and crossed swiftly into the changing room. He was due to take a women's self-defence class, and liked to be changed and ready in good time.

He leaned into his locker to get his gi – his judo suit – off his peg - and the lights went out.

Dressed in my little blue suit and tall pointed hat, I patrolled my manor. I strolled steadily down the cheerful High Street in the rich afternoon sunlight. I stopped off to talk to this one and that, and to keep an avuncular eye on the high jinks of the teenagers coming out of school, and eventually washed up at one of the local cafes to scrounge my free cup of tea and a bun. Not that it was scrounging; more symbiosis. The café owners are grateful for the occasional drop in by a copper. There was a tiny but rough element in the town – would-be small town Al Capones, every one - who would try and intimidate café owners, scrounge tea and buns make a general nuisance of themselves, and establish a protection racket. But not knowing when a copper would call in, especially one as big and ugly as me, acted as a definite cramp on their ambitions. Initially a few scuffles and arrests had been needed, but after a while, a hard, flat stare, perfected in my probationary attachment to Paddington Green nick in London -with a fairly-unofficial turnout or two with the SPG - sufficed. And most café owners thought a quiet, respectful clientele was worth a cup of tea and a bun. Plus, they liked to be seen nattering on good terms with the Old Bill.

I'd barely taken a bite out of my scone when my personal radio crackled into life; '215, Receiving?'

'215, Sarge, go ahead.'

'Bill, your mate PC Smith has just turned up at the sports centre, bleeding all over the carpet. He's been bashed on the noggin. He's asking for you. Wants to see you. ASAP' Despite the brisk uncaring words I knew Sergeant Watkins was like a mother hen with his lads.

'On my way, Sarge!'

Jogging down the high street, I espied a local teacher that I knew getting into her car.

'Mrs Giles, a favour please? Can you run me down to the Sports Centre quick as you like.'

'Sure, Bill, hop in!'

In I hopped, and had barely managed to shut the door when Mrs Giles did a tyre-howling U-turn and powered off as fast as her tired old Austin A30 would go.

'I've always wanted to do that! At least I can't be done for speeding with you here!' she grinned. But then, seriously, 'What's going on, William? What's the emergency?' turning a pupil-quelling eye on me, and I was again a squirming thirteen year old caught smoking behind the bike sheds.

'I don't really know…' I just stopped short of saying 'Miss.' 'All I know is that PC Smith has been attacked at the sports centre. He leads a women's self-defence class today.'

'I know John Smith; he came into school to tell my seniors why it's a good idea to stay legal and to stay fit. He had a wry and iconoclastic sense of humour, and the knowledge among the kids of his black belt didn't do any harm, either. The class loved him, all the lads wanted a black belt, and the girls went google-eyed.'

We screeched to a halt outside the sports centre, Hawaii 5-0 style, and rushed into the building. Mrs Giles followed me in, sweeping past the constable on duty. Not many in this town would gainsay her; she'd taught most of us.

And there, being cabbalistically muttered over by a hastily summoned doctor and two nurses, lay a very worse for wear Smithy. He had two black eyes and was bleeding copiously all down the back of his T-shirt. There was someone else's blood on the front of his shirt and all over his jeans as well. Incongruously, he was revealing mis-matched socks and was mumbling.

One of the centre attendants told me, 'He keeps saying "don't, Joe," and "led senses."' At that point, Smithy's eyes rolled up into his head and he lapsed back into a coma, still muttering.

I bent down and put an ear near him. 'That's 'Dojo,' the judo mat, and 'Dead Sensei' – that's the senior instructor. Dead. Let's go and have a look.' Propelling the poor centre girl ahead of me, we found the dojo. Nothing. 'Let's look in the changing room,' I gently requested her. As we came to the open door, she screamed. I motioned her behind me and looked in. There in the corner lay a shrivelled little old guy in a bloodstained judo suit.

'Don't come in, but run and get the attending constable, and the doctor as soon as he's finished with Smithy! Quick as you like!'

Sure enough, the little guy was dead. Very dead, with a cheap mass-produced kitchen knife still standing up horribly in his chest. Having seen Smithy safely and efficiently bandaged up by the doctor, taken the girl to the staff room and arranged a senior attendant to look after her, I told the attending detective, George Sargent, what little I knew and left the forensic team get on with it.

An ambulance clanged its way into the centre car park, laid Smithy on a trolley, and slapped a further temporary dressing on his head. Mrs Giles and I went in the ambulance with Smithy.

He was wheeled into a treatment room, his wound cleaned and dressed, his bloodstained clothes cut off, and one of those embarrassing bum-revealing surgical gowns squeezed onto him.

As the nurse went to put the garments in the bin, I hopped over, 'Keep those, please, Nurse, it's not all his blood! He got clobbered attending a very messy crime scene! They may be needed!'

When Smithy was put in a ward, Mrs Giles and I took turns to sit by him. What a way to spend your days off, I said to myself. We took turns, Mrs Giles marked books and I swotted for my sergeant's exam. Smithy just lay there with lots of things that went ping stuck in him.

It was a week before Smithy came round. I was on duty at the station when we got a phone call from the hospital and with Sarge's permission shot round there. Smithy was muttering and wriggling, gradually surfacing. When he regained consciousness, he was muttering the Twenty Third Psalm, 'Even though I walk through the valley of death I shall fear no evil…'

'Well, John, you certainly got close to that shadowy valley!' Mrs Giles said in best teacher manner, 'Don't you dare frighten us like that ever again!'

Smithy smiled, 'Sorry, Mrs Giles, must take up a better hobby.' Never lost his stupid sense of humour, that lad.

'Indeed you must! But now, we must find out who is responsible!'

I frowned at her, 'this is serious police stuff, Mrs Giles – and you're not Jane Marple. CID are working on it, but there has been no real progress,' I told them, 'There were no fingerprints on the knife that killed the sensei, the shotguns haven't been found, and there is no trace of what you, Smithy, could have been hit by, baseball bat, maybe.'

'Nunchuka,' breathed Smithy.

'You poor boy! Do you need a handkerchief?'

'No, Mrs Giles, I'm not sneezing, a nunchuka is a Japanese martial arts weapon, hinged like a flail, round like a baseball bat. The dojo is full of them.'

Inspector Forbes came to visit Smithy. Like most coppers a macabre sense of humour covered a deep compassion; 'Well, PC Smith. How are you feeling? It was a good job it was only your head they hit!'

Smithy tried to grin, but it turned into a grimace, 'Not too bad, thanks Inspector. Can't say I'll be on shift tomorrow!'

'We can put up without you for a while. Seriously, you concentrate on getting better. And can you bear a bit of questioning?'

'No problem, Sir. But I didn't see much. I went in to get ready for my ladies' self -defence course, and as I went to get into my locker, I was bashed on the bonce. I heard footsteps going away, but didn't see anyone. I sort of semi came round, and saw Sensei Akeni lying there with a dirty great knife stuck in him. I tested for pulse and breath; covering myself in his blood, and tried to crawl to get help. I fainted in the doorway and I believe some of my arriving ladies saw me and summoned help. Sorry that's all I know. Except I think the weapon may be a nunchuka, would CID check the dojo?'

'Thanks, Smith, will do. This is confidential between you and Watson,' Mrs Giles held her breath and went invisible, 'but as he was your teacher and friend, Smith, I will tell you about Sensei. He interrupted the bank raid that happened two weeks last Thursday. He intercepted one of the bandits, and tried to get his balaclava off, but was hit in the stomach and over the head with a gun barrel. He told me that he had something niggling in his brain about one of them; thought the robber looked like someone he knew, but couldn't put a finger on it. he promised he'd get in touch when something surfaced. In the meantime, you may have read that the robbers escaped - and that £5,000; the wages of Alawich's workers went with them. The manager went for the panic button and received both barrels at nil range. Autopsy's next Wednesday.'

At that moment, Mrs Giles left, returning in no time bearing a bag of home made cakes and gallons of Coke. Nodding a greeting to the inspector and me, she went straight up to Smithy and grinned, 'Well you don't look too bad today, considering you look like a panda in a turban! What's the diagnosis?'

'Cracked skull, I'm afraid. I'll be off for a lot of weeks, so please continue visiting and giving me all the scuttlebutt.'

'Really, anything at all I can do, don't hesitate. I'm retiring at the end of term; now on my third generation of the ratbags, and I feel I should give someone else a crack at 'em.'

I was sorry to hear that; she was a gold-standard teacher. She taught, she counselled, she cajoled, she laughed and wept with us. She was kind and she was stern, and commanded great respect, even from the ruffians like I had been. But above all she gave us a sense of self-worth and expectation. She was strict – oh boy, was she strict! But we always knew her motive was to fire us up. The school will miss her.

Mrs Giles, a force to be reckoned with; small, slim; sixty years old and still looked barely forty. Dressed usually in smart track suit and trainers. She still ran daily and did gymnastics three times a week. She had taught at Amplebury Grammar School for twenty nine years, as a PE teacher, swimming teacher and occasional English teacher. She had met her husband at Edge Hill College over in Lancashire and had been happily and sometime excitedly married for twenty five years to George, who had taught PE, woodwork and motor mechanics in Amplebury Secondary Modern – known affectionately by the kids but not to his face, as Farmer Giles - until a bout of double pneumonia brought on by falling off a cold, wet mountain and lying shivering for two hours until the Mountain Rescue team could fight their way up to him - had carried this fit, active man off.

When he died, both schools and most of the town had turned out to grieve with his widow.

'Sorry to hear you're retiring!' I nearly added 'Miss' again. 'The school and the town will miss you.'

'I'll miss the ratbags! But I won't miss staying up till midnight marking books, endlessly planning, and filling in forms to keep bureaucrats happy. About time I had a life for me. And that includes looking after you, Smithy. We never had any kids, so you'll have to do – you're appointed!'

And Smithy, all six-feet-how-much-of him actually simpered. I grinned at him behind her back.

'And you, young William! You're not getting away! You're one of my successes. You're going places!' then, shamefully, I simpered - and Smithy grinned. So it's true – teachers really do have eyes in the back of their heads.

The inspector stood up. 'Well, I'd better be off. But I'd better test one of those cakes; make sure they're all right for invalids.' And snaffling one, he left.

Mrs Giles leaned in. 'gather round, William. You are both coppers; John, your teacher was murdered. We must do something!'

'So, Mrs Giles, you mean a fund for his family? Something like that?'

'No, you great goon! We need to find out who did this. And please call me Amelia, you're no longer one of my Upper-sixth ratbags.' Amelia, the Velvet Steamroller.

I hummed and hawed, but Smithy leapt on it. 'Sure! I'll have a lot of time at home. And I taught Alawich's wife and the bank manager's wife self-defence. Two very nice families. I'm up for it!'

Finally, after much thinking and chewing over Queen' Regulations, I agreed. 'OK, but we must keep the inspector in the loop. He's a good guy; we play by the rules; we don't go behind his back, and if he says nay then nay it is.'

'Agreed!' they both chorused.

CHAPTER 2

The weeks passed. The police got nowhere with the robbery. We three got nowhere with the robbery. The police got nowhere with the murder. We three got nowhere with the murder. The reporters took less and less interest, until the story faded away. But Smithy slowly got better. The headaches eased, and the memory came back. His pastor and church members visited him regularly, pestered the hospital with phone calls, brought cakes, biscuits and chocolates round for him, and stayed nattering cheerily and promising to pray for him. His Self-Defence ladies visited him, also bringing cakes, chocolate and biscuits. And smuggled in a bottle of Red. Smithy was teetotal, so Amelia and I drank it in his honour. Smithy, Amelia and I put our heads together. We knew that Sensei had been niggled by something he recognised about one of the robbers, but hadn't managed to winkle it out of his brain. We kept the inspector up to date with lack of progress. He was a bit sceptical, but he said, 'You and Smith are coppers, and have a duty investigate. And Mrs Giles, shall we say, is a witness.' By the way he said 'Mrs Giles,' I realised that he too was in awe of her.

As I came out of his office, sniggers and whistles erupted from our tame CID Three Unwise Monkeys.

'How's your fwiend the Inthpector, *constable*?'

'Creep!'

'Sniveller!'

'Too good for us plebs then, Watson, me old mate?'

'How's about Teeecher, Watson? You and *Constable* Smith 'aving it off with Old Gilesey?'

'And how's your skiving God-bothering mate, Smithy? Still enjoying swinging the lead?'

Our three disenchanted, bone idle, gossipy CID warriors; a blot on the face of an otherwise keen, disciplined police station.

Shrugging, and fixing a gormless smile on my face, I strolled leisurely over, and stood, hands in pockets. Stopping in front of them, I dropped the gormless smile and adopted my flat, menacing stare.

'First off detective *constable* Godber, I am **not** your old mate! Never have been; never will be. I have standards.

'Secondly,' I continued, 'I do **not** creep. Never have, never will. And if I choose to report to the Shift Inspector, that is nothing to do with you idiots. So wind your necks in!

'Then again, you will not mucky the reputation of a fine teacher with your scummy comments. She is "Mrs Giles" to you! Try Respect!'

'Finally, my 'skiving mate' Smithy is off with a cracked skull. And even sitting watching telly, he's more active than you slugs!'

DC McLaren riposted, 'Clever bugger, aren't you, Watson?'

Johnson jeered, 'Getting nowhere with the Jap's murder are you, Plod? And you never will. Bet you've never even heard of the Alchemist!' McLaren sent him a 'shut up' glare. Interesting.

Johnson stuck his middle finger up at me, 'Ye're not worth the two!'

Still smiling, I reached over, picked him up by his very plain clothes lapels and shook him like the rat he was. I put him down courteously, smoothed his lapels, smiled and said, 'Anyone else?'

Shaking heads and mutters.

'Well then, I have a little game I've just made up to invite you join me in after shift. It's called cobble-diving. You put me down and I promise I won't intrude on your lacksadaisical useless so called investigation any more. I put you three down and you never again criticise me, Smithy or Mrs Giles. And you will stay out of my way. Respect, gentlemen, respect!

'And now I have a good old schoolyard dare for you.' I paused, patronisingly, 'Remember your colleague, PC Smith? fifth-Dan Judoka, self-defence trainer, the 'dare' is that you tell him to his face that you consider him a skiving God-botherer. Like all God-botherers, he's a peaceful dude, but how do you feel about challenging him? He might just teach you – practically, the hard way – some self-defence!'

I swanned over to my own desk humming 'Yabba-dabba-dabba Said the Monkey to the Chimp.'

End of shift. As I strolled into the car park at the back of the station, there were our three CID yobbos, grinning evilly. Johnson had a confiscated flick knife, McLaren his truncheon and Godber a set of brass knuckles.

Divide and conquer, I told myself, *Flick knife first.*

I backed towards the exit, trying to look timorous. As expected, the Three Wise Monkeys spread out to cover it. I swung towards Johnson, grabbing his outstretched flick knife arm and twisted. Hard enough to hear a wrist dislocate.

Spinning round I kicked Mclaren on the shin. Safer and I'm less off-balance than going for the groin. As he bent over, I grabbed his truncheon and hit his elbow with it. Something gave!

Godber, seeing me between him and the exit, panickedly punched his brass knucks at me. Ducking under them, I roundhoused him in the solar plexus, following up with a left cross to the nose. He too found the asphalt.

'Well, now lads, shame it came to that,' I paused to take a breath or two, 'we're supposed to be on the same side. But how about you lot getting out and trying investigating? When you're better, of course,' I solicitously crooned, 'And now you can all join Skiving Smithy on his couch! AFTER you've been to the emergency ward!'

I looked up to hear a round of applause. Incoming shift and outgoing shift alike cheering and clapping. ''Bout time those useless goons got some comeuppance!' someone yelled.

Said useless goons crept out, wounded in body and pride.

Then I saw the inspector at his window, beckoning with crooked finger. I smartened up immediately and expected the rousting of the century followed by instant dismissal. I rushed up the stairs, knocked on his door, and on the command Come, crashed in, coming smartly to attention, helmet under arm.

'Watson, my lad. I'm afraid that behaviour constitutes an official reprimand and will go down on your record as a disagreement with colleagues that resulted in horseplay. Now the reprimand, Watson... that was very naughty! Don't do it again!'

I sighed with relief, expecting to be ex-PC Watson.

Then, relaxing, Forbes said, 'I do **not** want you to be a snout or Inspector's Boy, but – and this must go no further than Smithy or Mrs G – I suspect something of the reek of old haddock about at least one of them. I've got my eye on them. Keep yours open. The Superintendent knows my suspicions. Now stumm! Dismissed!'

Phew!

I went round to see Smithy.

He was contentedly sitting up, munching grapes. Mrs G – Amelia - was perched on the end of the bed, tanned face and arms contrasting strongly with Smithy's pale ghostliness.

'What have you been up to, William? I remember that look from your playground scraps!'

So I quickly unfolded my version of practical self-defence training. Amelia looked at me, raised her eyebrows and sighed. Smithy said, 'Good on you, Bill. You know I'm a pacifistic sort of guy, but those three have been throwing their weight about among the youth; dragging in quite harmless kids in 'for questioning.' And my reputation is meek and mild; airy-fairy, is it? must disabuse them.'

Smithy is a gentle guy; both his Christian principles and his judo training leads to gentleness and respect for others. But gentle isn't soppy. And I felt sorry for our three idiots.

Then we settled down to serious discussion. Amelia had asked her sixth-formers if they had heard any gossip, and Smithy had enquired of his church people – the ones that ran the soup kitchen and drop-in centre in the town if there had been any scuttlebutt amongst the clients. We just got vague whispers that something was not right under the town's placid countenance.

'Have you heard of The Alchemist?' I asked Amelia, 'It's something one of the three wise monkeys mentioned. And the looks he got from the others, I gather it is very much under wraps.'

I promised too that I too would ask about among my contacts and snouts. Then Amelia and I left.

CHAPTER 3

I continued around my beat, nose sniffing busily for all wrongdoing but especially for any whiff about Sensei's murderer or the robbery. Like Smithy, Sensei had been a gentle guy; very interested in giving the town youth a focus and ambition, at a time when teenage Teddy-boy gangs were beginning to make waves in the town. He had brought a sense of self-worth to those of all ages in his club, and strongly insisting to the more exuberant teen lads that there will be no fighting off the dojo. The town had looked on him as a sort of mascot and were deeply offended and angered by his murder. But not a whisper about who had killed him.

Then, a couple of weeks later, as I passed an alleyway between shops; 'Pssst! Mr Watson!'

I turned cautiously, expecting trouble. A round yokel-head peered out. Bill Boyd; a town ne'er-do-well. He was a happy hooligan with a lousy family background, a penchant for other's property and a stunted moral growth. But in an odd sort of way, I liked the idiot.

'Come in 'ere! I can't be seen talking to you!'

Senses alert, fingering truncheon, I eased in. He was alone.

'Don't let this get out! Promise!' Boyd muttered out of the side of his mouth, best gangster style, 'Don't take it back to the station. I don't trust your CID!' *Who does?* I thought.

'Let's hear it.'

'You're a straight 'un. We all know that. And you let me off that shoplifting charge, I feel I owe yer.'

I had lifted him for a very amateur attempt to nick a second hand watch, worth less than a quid from a second-hand shop. It would have cost

14

more than that in my time and in court fees to bust him. So I shook him gently, snarled at him, and with the shopkeeper's agreement, sent him off with a flea in his ear to work Saturdays in the shop. He worked hard and honest on Saturdays, but was still a scally the rest of the week.

'I didn't do judo, but all us lads respected him. We want his killer caught – it'll take the heat off us! 'he grinned ruefully. 'But there's a whisper going around that there's a character come in the town who's trying to take over – stuff we wouldn't touch; drugs, fencing – and there's a rumour that there's a knocking shop in town. Right seedy flat above the chippy.'

'How would you know?' I enquired teasingly. Boyd reddened.

'Just kidding. Any more''

'Funny moniker – calls himself something-mist. Bit like chemist.'

Disguising my pricked-up ears, I thanked him gravely, and dashed him a ten-bob note.

CHAPTER 4

When I got off shift, I rang Amelia and she agreed we would meet around Smithy's bed and discuss what to do about this 'something-mist.' As we walked into the ward, there was a good-looking nurse sat on the end of Smithy's bed. They were heads together in deep conversation. I whistled a meaningless tune and Amelia developed a ladylike frog in the throat. The nurse jumped up. Change 'good looking' for 'startlingly beautiful.' Tall, slim, long blonde hair escaping from nurse's cap. And stacked.

'I'm glad your blood pressure is fine, Mr Smith!' she carolled, bustling away.

'Blood pressure fine, Smithy?' I enquired solicitously, 'You can't be well – mine would be 220/170 being so near that gorgeous creature!'

'That's Alicia. I taught her as a grubby eleven-year old tomboy,' contributed Amelia.

'She goes to the same church as me,' Smithy told us lamely.

'Yes, I thought you'd be discussing theology,' I grinned. 'Anyway, glimmer of light on the murder of Sensei. Remember I told you about one of CID eejits mentioning an alchemist? Well, one of my regular customers down the nick has just told me of a major team moving into the area; led by a 'something-mist,' and I've been wondering.'

'It's a pity our CID is decidedly iffy, or we could have chatted them up about it.' mused Smithy.

'And I don't think any of my school hooligans move in those sorts of circles,' from Amelia.

Stymied, we turned to other topics. Amelia kept us laughing with some of the howlers from her younger classes; Francis Drake circumcised the world in a forty-foot cutter; Jesus' mother was called Mary Christmas and the works of Shakespeare weren't written by Shakespeare but by another man of the same name.

Smithy was finally sprung from hospital and sent home with strict orders to do nothing for at least a month. I continued foot patrols. I continued keeping the Inspector in the loop. And CID out of it. And the NHS reported that drug-involved and drink-fuelled cases in Emergency had risen by over a hundred and ten percent in the last year. And CID just couldn't get a handle on the problem. Funny, that.

I kept pestering all my 'customers' for any news, but all seemed fearful and unwilling to talk; even unwilling to be seen near me.

Then one evening the nick was notified that William Boyd, Scoundrel of this Parish had been admitted to hospital with multiple wounds. I made a point of getting over there as soon as I could. And in the Emergency ward, I found Johnson and McLaren gathered around his bed, bullyragging him. A harassed nurse ineffectually tried to demand rest for him, and that they should leave.

'Get lost, Sweetheart. This is police business!'

I strolled in, 'Evening, Lads, you're working late! Been locked out at home? Missus down the Bingo…or *somewhere?*'

'Get lost, Watson. Take your pointed head somewhere else. Ever heard of CID? This is our business.'

I smiled, and mused thoughtfully, 'CID? CID? I vaguely remember there used to be one in the nick, Oh! I Remember, Clowns in Disguise? Cops in Disgrace?' then muttered just in their hearing, 'Car park? Again soon, maybe?' and went and lifted Johnson out of his chair and sat proprietorially on it. That was not easy, Johnson was a big lad, and tended to the porky.

Johnson scowled and sneered, 'Don't go away, Boyd. We'll be back.'

I waited until their rear elevations were out of the ward, then, 'So, Bill me lad, what happened to you?'

'It were a car, Mr Watson. A car. An' it din't stop'

'Hmm,' I mused, 'sure it wasn't Boadicea's chariot – the one with the knives on the wheels?'

'Wot?'

'Strange car to give you those cuts on your face. Could be mistaken for razors. The bruises I could just about accept. But not those cuts!'

'It were a car! 'E should be reported! Dangerous driving!' and he wouldn't budge, rolling scared-rabbit eyes all round the ward.

'OK, Boyd, if that's the way you want it. but take care. You're looking run down!' He was not amused, but chuckling at my own joke, I strolled out.

Time passed. Smithy slowly recovered, mothered, looked after and kept in order by Amelia. I went round there regularly and talk naturally turned to the robbery and murder. And Amelia kept us well fuelled on grub; her stews, pasties and cake would be worth crawling over broken bottles for. And as a cook, Smith varied between merely awful and disgusting. Amelia's offering this evening was a new to these shores from Italy; a lasssag-something. I couldn't pronounce it, but I managed to run to two helpings. Poor little stick-thin damaged Smithy managed three. And it was followed by Lemon Meringue pie. I sighed, replete, "Amelia, if you weren't my ex-teacher, a bit older than me, and if I wasn't scared stiff of you, I'd offer to marry you!"

'Stupid boy, Watson!' she growled, but with a twinkle.

We settled down to discuss, 'this Alchemist idiot…' mused Amelia, 'Why do all these criminal idiots give themselves silly nicknames? I blame Edgar Wallace and all those thirties writers, myself.'

'I wonder…' I mused, 'Alchemist?…Chemist?…is it too obvious? We have a new dispenser down at the chemist's. maybe I'll go and have a look. Can't do any harm; may spark something.'

Sensei's judo club reopened after the funeral. But not like it was before. The new sensei, Ernest Wilson, like Smithy, was a fifth dan, but older. But he did not follow in Akeni's footsteps. He was approaching middle aged, just beginning to get grey hair on his temple. He was about five foot eight, stocky and very muscular with a face like a bag of hammers. He was hard, brutal, both on the judo-mat and off it, determined to take the club into competition; determined to get trophies, determined to get a name in the judo world. And totally dismantling the sense of honour and respect that Sensei had inculcated. Unfortunately, there will always be go-getters and bully-boys in every sporting endeavour. Sensei Akeni had kept these in control, and tried to bring the honour of The Gentle Way into the club's psyche. Wilson encouraged them to go all out for victory, regardless of the time-honoured ethics of Judo, stressing that winning was all. Many of the club left, in fear or disgust.

Smithy was dozing gently in front of a crackling fire when the doorbell rang. He levered himself awake, levered himself up, and made his doddering way to the front door. There, looking agitated stood George MacIver, a twenty-one year old first dan from the club.

'Smithy…is it OK if I call you Smithy?'

'Call me anything you like but don't call me too late for lunch.'

George smiled hesitantly; uncertainly. 'Smithy, I need someone to talk to.'

'Come on in, Lad, can I offer you a coke? Some tea?'

Perched on the edge of an upholstered chair and picking nervously at the fabric on an arm, George began, diffidently, embarrassed. 'I am not a stoolie. I don't like talking about people in authority behind their backs, but I am seriously worried about the club. The new sensei, Mr Wilson, is not like Sensei Akeni.'

'I take it that your problem is more than a difference in style.'

Gaining confidence, MacIver elaborated, 'There have been injuries, one or two quite serious. There has been bullying, sneering at those a bit unsure. Going too rough on the younger and less experienced. And his physical exercise is crippling. I know Sensei was tough – I've never been so exhausted in my life than after some of his sessions, but he was caring. He pushed us to the limit but never beyond. And he was always encouraging and never scathing if you couldn't do something. He would lead you and demonstrate until you could. He gave you an end in view. This guy never lets up, although he doesn't do the training himself. Just bellows from the edge of the dojo. And failure gets a tongue lashing or you get held up to ridicule in front of everyone. And there are some very dodgy characters joined the club, Wilson's Private Army, we call them. Some of the old club have left, and when they do, he gloats, telling us he doesn't want softies and jessies in his club. HIS club, mark you! I hate it! if I hadn't qualified for a place in the Nationals, I'd have gone!'

'Anybody else feel that way?'

George produced a packet of letters from his capacious anorak pocket. 'The lads and lasses didn't want to come as a mob to pester you while you're recovering. These are get-well letters from the club, but there are also some grave concerns in there.'

Smithy quickly perused some. Jimmy, knee dislocated by an unnecessarily rough throw was told to get up and stop being a wimp. Young Clare, seven stone and four-foot-and-a-fag-end tall, suffering a juji-jime choke by a large member of Wilson's Army until she went blue, despite tapping to be released. 'And the worst thing,' she had written, 'is that he was really enjoying strangling me. I won't go there again!' the list went on, deploring the state that Sensei's club had gone down to.

'OK, thanks, George, as I can't get to see him, I will write to him. Now, what would you say to tea and a piece of Mrs Giles' cake?'

'I'd say, "hello, tea and Mrs Giles' cake!"' quipped George, good nature restored that he had got it off his chest, and thankful that Smithy believed him.

CHAPTER 5

As soon as George had gone, Smithy got out Amelia's best Basildon Bond notepaper and second-best fountain pen and wrote;

Dear Ernest, I am sure that in taking Sensei's
club over, you have its best interests
at heart. Yet it has come to my attention that
you are being perhaps a little too
forceful to some of the younger and less experienced.
I feel it my duty to remind you of the values of honour
and mutual respect that Sensei taught and lived.

Regards.
John.

A reply came by return of post;

Dear Constable Smith,
Thank you for your letter. However I am now Sensei of this club,
officially appointed by the Judo Council, and have
carte blanche to run the club in my way.
I feel that Akeni was far too lenient on the softies,
the skivers and those playing at judo.
I intend to make this club a name to be reckoned with.
Finally, Smith, I have withdrawn your membership
of the club on the grounds of ill-health.

You have no jurisdiction, and should you try to enter these premises, I will have you escorted off as a trespasser,

Yours,

E Wilson, Sensei

When Smithy showed Amelia and me the letter, she was incandescent. Smithy said, 'I don't mind the insult to me. I'm used to that as a copper, but to think that the club that Sensei put so many years into, and so much care, makes me want to throttle him!'

And that from pacifist Christian Smithy really was something.

'Well!...The cheek of the man! So, when we sort out Sensei's murder, we will take that arrogant middle-aged Hitler down a peg or two!' Amanda was on her high horse. Miss Marple on amphetamines. And Amelia had had forty years taking arrogant teenagers and parents down a peg or two. I briefly felt sorry for Wilson. But only briefly.

'Enough of me,' Smithy smiled grimly, 'Back to our *moutons*. Watching telly and reading had given me a lot of time to think. And someone famous said, "follow the money," and this all started when the money left. It was the money that got the bank manager and Sensei murdered. So, Bill, could you approach Forbes for a scan of bank details?'

'I will indeed, I'm on mornings tomorrow. and I'll respectfully request that he sidelines CID. There's something very smelly about those three – and I don't mean their beer breath!'

Two hundred miles away, Little Joe Rollings sat fearfully in his borrowed bedsit. He needed to get out of London pretty fast for health reasons. Reasons that could end up being given an extra smile with a cut-throat razor. Or a pair of tastefully broken legs. Or even with a new residence in concrete under a newly-building council house. He had seriously annoyed the Sheldon Brothers; totally amoral East End gangsters; total psychopaths, and he needed to be somewhere – anywhere – else. He had precipitously left his posh flat on top of an old but well looked after three storey town house. He had left his black Rover Ninety. And he had left his sharp suits, cool shirts and oxfords. Thankfully one of his former pimps had given him the heads up that the Sheldons were coming round to see him – personally.

So he scarpered. Thankfully he had a bit of cred left with one of his toms, Daphne Doors, (Real name Maisie Billings.) He ran to her pad. she accepted him – but not overnight. She didn't want her face carving. So, packing his few belonging in the tatty cardboard suitcase he had nicked off the market, he got ready to set out to Euston Station to start a new life as a Criminal Mastermind.

'I don't know why they took against me so much!' he moaned to her, 'There's plenty of scope for a small firm like mine. Bit of gentle drug pushing to Lascar sailors off the ships; running a few toms on only one street. But you're my favourite; you're my girl! Bit of local enforcing on shopkeepers. Nothing getting in Rupert and Richard's way! It's greed! They just want everythin'. But me first lieutenant 'as gone sick with a baseball bat shaped 'eadache. And me other lot are gone. Just gone! And a mate givin' me the bad news that the Sheldons have marked my card. And even you can't put me up!' He nervously lit his last Woodbine, brushed the ash off his cavalry-twill-copy trousers and reached for her road atlas.

'Where to go?' he mused.

'What about Blackpool?' She suggested, 'It's a jumping place in summer, lots of Northern oiks on holiday, all "ee-bah-gum," and ready for a bit of what you can give 'em. I had a holiday there once with me aunty. Got off with a guy from Bolton; lovely big muscles from all that factory humping, but thick as a plank. Spent a fortune on me, 'e did. But I saw to it he got good value!'

Little Joe scratched his none too clean but slicked back and Brylcreemed head, disturbing a cloud of sticky dandruff and his mind settled on Blackpool. He had once had his only holiday as a kid when Social Services had taken him for a week to see the lights. He had loved it, loved playing on the beach, splashing in the sea, and scaring himself on the fairground. He wished he was back in those days.

'Well, not Blackpool,' he pondered, 'Too busy. Too many holiday makers. The Underworld will be set up already.' (he always thought of what he did as The Underworld.)

Maise spoke up, 'But there's a small town near there, maybe. A yokel small town out in the sticks...where?...where?...How's about

Bradkirk-on-the-Eller! The Sheldons will never think of you there! Population about twenty thousand, main work on the local farms…bit of factory work. Full of hayseeds.'

Joe perked up. 'Bet I can make a go of things out there! come with me!'

'Not on yer Nellie!" she riposted. "All them lumbering yokels sayin' Eyup. I belong in the Smoke! A week there'd drive me mad.'

'What about the Sheldons?'

'I'm OK with them. Doin' a bit in their clubs. It's you they want, not me! Anyway they know you're here. They're on their way!'

'Did you shop me?'

''Course I did. A girl's got to live. And I do mean *live!*'

He gasped at her disloyalty and infidelity. His favourite whore! Letting him down and selling him out. Putting his very life risk. So, smacking her in the mouth, he grabbed his bag and fled, banging the door as hard as he could on her foul mouthed imprecations.

Thankfully, he saw a taxi, just in time as a black Ford V8 Pilot was pulling up. Jumping in, he gasped, 'Euston Station! Quick as yer like! I'm late! Or I could be,' with grim humour. He got there and scuttled like a rabbit into the Liverpool Express. Just in time to see a black V8 Pilot drew onto the station forecourt.

When he stopped gasping and his heart stopped threatening to jump out of his chest and wriggle round the floor, he took stock. Sipping his thick white mug of the Thames sludge that BR liked to call coffee, and recovering his arrogance, he planned. He had read crime novels assiduously when in Borstal. Raymond Chandler…Edgar Wallace…Leslie Charteris… and all their criminals had nicknames…the Black Shadow, the Thin Man, The Spider. The Saint! So he needed a nickname…'What do I call myself to impress these country hicks?…the Shadow…the Sharp Boy…' He reflected. Then the light came on. He had worked a few Saturdays as a teenager brushing up in Timothy White's the chemist. So - 'The Alchemist! Yes! Sounds mysterious. Sounds clever; somebody who can do things! And I can! I could have in London. But if only those scumbag Sheldons had left me alone. I'll have this place sewn up in no time! Again he moaned at his lot – exiled in clog-and-shawl land. Just 'cos two psychopaths wanted his little business.

Sitting on the train, he continued to plan. *OK, so how to start the mysteriousness?* he pondered. Thankfully, he had money from his nefarious London activities, he had had a good education; local grammar school then Further Education college. He had managed eight 'O' levels and got a City & Guilds in Accountancy and English. So he wasn't stupid like those nasty Sheldons; all brute force and ignorance, and he wasn't stupid like those hayseeds he was moving into.

First off, get a good drum, he mused, *Should get a flat easy enough. Then a good car. Reckon I can get one cheap. Live outside of that naff little town, so I don't get noticed.*

The train pulled into the noisy, steamy coal-messy vault of Liverpool Lime Street station. He collected his tatty suitcase, *Soon be able to buy real leather!* he grinned to himself. He surrendered his ticket, and hailed a taxi to take him across town to Exchange Station. Looking out of the window, he had a brainwave. He saw in the gathering darkness, lots of 'ladies' outside Lime Street, each with a red-lit torch on display. *Whores!* He thought. *And no Sheldons to upset my applecart! I bet Bradkirk hasn't got any. And I bet the busies are thick yokels! Bet I can set up a nice little roadhouse just off the A59."*

He bought a ticket for Blackpool, and with much chuffing and puffing, the train lumbered away toward his new better life."

CHAPTER 6

'Follow the money!' repeated Smithy. *'Cui Bono?'*

'What?' I gurgled. 'Queue where?'

Amelia's schoolteacher persona surfaced. 'It's Latin, Bill. Means who's benefitting. Who's got the money? Literally, who's it good for.'

'I'll try and persuade Forbesy to get a court order for the bank,' I said.

'Let me have a go,' Smithy asked. 'I'm up and about again,' and receiving one of Amelia's classroom-quelling looks, 'Well, nearly. And I will be by tomorrow. I knew the manager well socially; I taught his wife self-defence. And both children of the assistant manager. He held both his boss and Sensei Akeni in highest regard. And we're a small backwater with a small backwater branch. I think he'll help.'

Inspector Forbes was a copper's copper. Not promoted beyond his ability; in fact he had turned down promotion to stay in what he called 'real policing.' And out of the thin atmosphere of bureaucracy and small town politics.

Much argument followed; Smithy versus me and Amelia; this wasn't strictly legal; the Assistant Manager could get into trouble, and anyway, Smithy, you've never been out of the house!

But Smithy is a stubborn toad, and when he gets an idea in his head it takes dynamite to shift it. He heard us out, one eyebrow raised, and then said, 'Amelia, will you pick me up at half past nine?'

Amelia sighed, muttered something about I wish I had you in my class for half an hour, then resignedly sighed again, 'Oh, I suppose so, you stubborn lump! And if you drop dead don't come running to me!'

Next morning, suitably dressed in mufti, with a carefully-arranged turban of bandage prominently displayed, leaning on his cane and with Amelia as duty nurse holding one arm and clucking sub voce, he tottered into the nick. Greeting Sergeant Hailey on the desk, he carolled, 'Morning George. Mr Forbes in?' Hailey beamed, "Well…look who's been dug up! Good to see you Smith!' He lifted his internal receiver and grinned, 'Guess who's here to see you, Sir! PC Smith! Looks like a Turk in his turban, and he's got his minder with him! But he's upright and moving!' Putting the receiver down, he grinned, 'Go on up! He'll be glad to see you! You too, Mrs Giles.'

On his way up to the Inspector's office, he noticed the three scions of the CID busily doing nothing as usual. I was watching from the side lines – also busy doing nothing. But I was proud of the lad. He walked straight up to them, and smiling beatifically crooned 'Goood morning, gentlemen. A little bird tells me – in fact a hulking great big bird tells me that you three scions of the establishment consider me a skiving God-botherer. And…as you can see, this skiving God-botherer is still with us. Now…here I am and here I will be full time again soon. And I may only be a lowly PC, and not an exalted Detective…but, I am asking you nicely not to get in my way. My sensei was very dear to me – like a father – and I intend to seek his killers – if necessary in my own time. Now I am asking nicely because I am very concerned.'

'What are *you* concerned about, *Constable?*' sneered Johnson.

'to be honest, Johnny-boy, I am concerned about your health. Dare I mention a certain car park? PC Watson is a very able scrapper, but I am a scientist. And I teach Martial Arts. Would you care for a lesson?'

'What? In *your* state??' incredulously.

'I never boast or claim to be better than I am; Sensei could tie me in knots. But rest assured, gentlemen, even in this state I could take all three of you – and will if I need to. And one last thing, you will never refer to this lady with me in any derogatory terms. Car park, anyone? All this given in a quiet conversational tone, with a peaceable little smile, 'And furthermore any laxatives in my tea or nasties left in my locker, I will be round for a quiet word with you three. In fact, you better wish no one leaves a pencil for me to trip over. Goodbye!'

'Here, you lowly blue-pointed-head copper, you can't talk to us like that!'

'Oh? I thought I just had done. And please believe me, I never threaten, and I never make promises I can't keep. So please defend my Christian conscience and your health by not upsetting me.'

No answer just sullen looks.

Just then, Inspector Forbes stood at the top of the stairs, 'Come on, Smith! No time for social chatter!' he smiled like a shark at dinner time.

When Smithy and Amelia were seated in his visitors' chairs, Forbes began, 'How are you, Smith? Wound healing OK? Have you still got a couple of brain cells intact?' He rang down for coffee, then continued, 'What of emergency importance brings you off your sick-bed, when you categorically shouldn't be?'

'Well, Sir, I have had lots of time to cogitate and have been busily stretching the brain to see if anything comes up about the bank-robbery and murder.' He hastily continued, 'I know it's not my case, Sir, I'm still on sick leave, and I don't want to detract from the investigation, but Amelia and Bill and I have talked a lot about it and the idea came, *follow the money*. I was wondering if any bank details have been made available to the police?'

'We made enquiries via the head office, but they were not prepared to open their accounts without a financial search warrant. Which the Super wasn't prepared to do.'

'In that case, I was wondering, as I knew the manager very well, and the whole bank staff knows me with my self defence training, if I were to approach the assistant manager, whom I also know very well and is still grieving his boss – if I approached him - just man-to-man. It wouldn't be as a PC, how could it be? I'm on extended sick leave!'

Forbes gave a quirky smile. 'Of course, I can't possibly authorise you to do that, Smith, it could be serious trouble for you, the acting manager – and me! So don't you dare let me hear of you doing any such thing. And if the bank complained I would have to severely reprimand you. All I want to hear is that you are at home recovering. And, Watson, stop lurking behind my door. Come in, I need an update on your work, Watson.' And it so happened that there was coffee and biscuits involved. He is a crafty ratbag is our inspector.

On our way out, Smithy noticed that Johnson & Co were giving one of the few station WPCs a hard time. She was blushing furiously, held by McLaren's ugly great paw. Before I could intervene, Smithy went over; 'Hello, Miss, I'm PC Smith of this parish, currently being on sick leave. I'm a bit out of touch, I wonder if you would show me to the crew room – I've quite forgotten.' As we walked away I whispered 'Car park!'

She smiled thankfully as McLaren let go of her arm, 'I'm Helen Doughty, just moved here from Preston. And I haven't been overly impressed by my welcome.'

'A bit overwhelming a welcome, I would have thought,' I said, 'But I hope the rest of the lads are OK?'

'Usual banter, but no different from how they chaff each other. So I feel part of the team. Apart from those slimeballs. I won't tell you the sort of sick stuff they were saying.'

Smithy excused himself, and limped back to the CID patch. 'Helen now is out of bounds to you three.'

'She can't take a bit of banter'" grunted Godber, 'She'll never make it as a copper. Only after the men!'

'I doubt that, but the worst whore on Liverpool Lime Street doesn't deserve your slime. Two more words for you to consider. The first – car. The second – park. *Leave her alone!*'

'Well said, Smithy!' crowed Amelia, 'I always thought you were far too placid and religious to get so warlike.'

'Normally I am,' mused Smithy, 'but such misuse of authority makes my blood boil. And I think that as a Christian, I'm supposed to be against all forms of bullying and advantage-taking. And those three have a very peculiar smell – and I don't mean their socks and stale breath. I mean, oh, how can I put it? There is a stink of something worse there than just lousy coppering. Those three are up to something.'

The neon sign flickered its dubious message into the evening air, **The Ace of Clubs.** Richard and Rupert lounged on a leather sofa each, looking through the one-way glass at the monkeys cavorting below. Rupert was flicking idly through a very rare and discreet magazine specially imported from Amsterdam. Richard was cleaning his fingernails with a flick knife. Both had their dark grey suit jackets off and their noisy ties undone.

A discreet knock came on the door. A muscular thug opened the door, and announced, 'Daffy to see yer, gents,' ushering Daphne in. she was undersized and scraggy with straggly blonde hair, not a bit like the Diana Dors she sought to emulate.

'Come in, Sweet'eart, pour yerself a drink. Siddown.' Grunted Rupert.

'An' how did it go?' from Richard.

''E swallered it hook line an' sinker! Panicking like yer'd never believe!'

'And we saw him off at Euston – just let the V8 wave him goodbye!' chortled Richard. 'And here's yer twenty-five quid, Daf. Now what we want you to do next, is keep in touch with him. Ring him regular – coupla times a week. Maybe go and see him sometimes. Fiver a phone call, fifty quid plus expenses for a visit. Encourage him to set up a scam up in Bugtussle-in-the-Marsh or whatever that woollyback place is called.'

'Why are yer doin' this? It's way out of your manor?'

'We shouldn't be telling you this, but yer a good girl, and can keep yer mouth shut, but we have a friend in a high place – a very high place, who wants to get big in Lancashire. Lots of trade in the coastal resorts. We don't want to move, so we thought of Little Joe – not doing our business any harm, but windy – scared of his own shadow.'

'And certainly scared of us!' broke in Rupert, 'So we thought we'd send him up there to set up – you were very useful there, Daffy Duck!'

Swallowing her annoyance at being addressed so, Daphne said, 'I guess there's money in it?'

"More than you can imagine, Daf! Wheelbarrows of the stuff. Enough to give us a Roller each and light our cigars with fivers. And if you carry on being a good girl, you might just get enough to run barefoot through the fivers! Nah go an' get yourself a bop downstairs. And the whisky's on the house!'

Lord Lucas stretched out, he was dressed in dazzlingly blue silk pyjamas and paisley dressing gown. *Just got rid of the whore, so just got time for a phone call before Maggie gets home from her goody-goody charity stuff.*

He reached out a long arm for the telephone and dialled a number he knew well.

'Ace Club.'

'It's me.'

'Wotcher, yer Lordship,' sardonically answered Richard.

Lucas swallowed an angry retort. These unschooled East End plebs ought to give him more respect. But you have to work with what you can get. And these two were well connected in Gangsterland – and quite fearsome. 'Has the pigeon flown?'

'Yer, gone up Blackpool way. An' we've still got contact.'

'Good lads, two-fifty will get into your bank tomorrow.' hanging up abruptly, he redialled. 'Nigel, it's me. How are you? Have the brats settled down at Eton?'

'Brats settled well, thanks, Lukey. You keeping well?'

'Just bought a share in a shooting lodge outside Aviemore. Bit run down and the natives are very uncouth; hairy Jocks, but the peasant-shooting's good.' They both chuckled at the old joke. Old Etonians together. 'But now to business. Have your friends got a consignment coming in?'

'On their way. Should be able to deliver about fifty to Morecambe Bay within a month. And a few packages.'

'What are they? Chinks? Blacks? Krauts?' Thus spoke one who is certain of his aristocracy, his education and his Englishness.

'I believe the Americans call them gooks – refugees from Vietnam.'

Next day, Smithy ably helped by Mrs Giles hobbled into the bank. 'I wonder, could I have a word with Jeff Tomkins?'

'I'm afraid he's a bit busy at the moment, but if you would make an appointment…?'

Smithy smiled courteously, 'Would you tell him I'm John Smith, and I teach his wife self-defence?'

'Oh, you're *that* John Smith, the injured copper!'

'I am, but strictly not on police business. As you can see, I'm still on sick leave.'

Within a minute Jeff Tomkins ushered Smithy and Amelia into his office. He did not look like a bank-manager. He was tall and broad, boxed at Cambridge, got his rugby blue, joined the Paras and got medically discharged with nothing more heroic than a drunken pongo driving a landrover into him and neatly removing his right leg.

'So, *Mr* Smith,' very formally but with a mischievous grin, 'what can I do you for? And Mrs Giles. Heard you'd retired. How goes it?'

'Fine, apart from having to nursemaid this long lanky victim.' Amelia had taught Jeff.

Then down to business. 'This is very unofficial, but I wonder could we have a look at some bank accounts? It can't be official because our Super reckons we haven't enough evidence for a search warrant. And the money from the bank robbery hasn't turned up, or been spent – at least not locally – so we are looking for any iffy deposits have been made.'

'Oh, I'm really sorry, Smithy, I couldn't possibly show you those – it's more than my job's worth. And in a minute, I have to go down to the vault, and the last quarter's deposit and withdrawal forms are on the desk. Now you *must not* under any circumstances open that confidential folder. I shall be only five minutes, then we can have a coffee together.'

Like an eagle swooping on an unfortunate lamb, Amelia had the folder open and was riffling through it, muttering and writing with a miniature pencil in a little note book. There was a rattle of coffee cups from outside the door, and Jeff came in followed by a motherly-looking middle aged lady bearing a tray. 'Hope you can force a bit of Victoria sponge,' she beamed. We chatted inconsequentially for a while, revelling in the coffee and cake, then made our farewells.

As soon as we got down the street, Amelia whooped, waved a little notebook in the air and did a most unteacherly dance on the pavement.

When she had finished behaving like a banshee on amphetamines, she said, 'As soon as Bill gets off shift, we will have a good old look at what I have here. I think it will be very enlightening! Let me treat you two to dinner at a restaurant, you must be sick of four walls, Smithy.' Her objection to Smithy being out and about seemed to have vanished.

Little Joe soon settled into bucolic life. His fear of the Sheldons now belonged to an entirely different life. He moved into a fairly decent flat in Blackpool, quite a way from the Golden Mile, and so quite cheap and anonymous. He transferred his bank account to the National in Blackpool, and found he still had enough capital to set up in Bradkirk. He found a flat above one of the town centre chippies, decorated it on the cheap like a 1900's Paris bordello, all pink and flouncy, and after a bit of careful sounding out which whore had a pimp and which hadn't, he recruited a few – his London accent and past experience stood him in good stead, and inveigled a few of them to do some shift work in Bradkirk. It was a slow beginning but after a while the local farm youths in their Teddy-boy suits began to find his establishment a good end to a Saturday night out. Looking at their thick-soled footwear, Joe remarked to himself, *Now I know why they're called brothel-creepers.*

Then after a while those middle-aged middle class gentlemen whose wives thought *sex* was what the upper crust kept coal in also found their way to the chip shop. Which gave Little Joe lots of blackmail material. Nothing too obvious, just the odd favour.

At the end of my shift, I got an urgent message at the nick from a Mrs Sykes that I was needed at the Barleycorn; the poshest restaurant in town, ASAP. So hurrying home to shower and change out of uniform, I dashed round there. I was greeted by a grinning pair of co-conspirators. 'We'll order first, then go into the lounge for coffee and conspiracy,' beamed Amelia, 'And this is my treat for a hardworking copper and a poor suffering invalid.'

We tucked in. Prawn cocktails for me and Smithy, breaded mushrooms for Amelia. Then sirloin medium rare for me, whilst Smithy had a double Chateaubriand, and Amelia a large Beef Wellington. Followed by apple pie and whisky cream all round. I thought I was a hearty trencherman, but those two skinny wretches…!

Ordering coffee, we decamped to the lounge. Amelia reached into her capacious handbag and brought out a small notebook. 'Look at this!' she crowed. 'Look at certain names. Over the last three months, look at how much our delightful detectives have socked away.' We looked over her shoulder. It was an extra £50 a month. A whacking great addition to their pay packets. 'I wonder what they have to do for that… pondered Amelia. 'And look at this!' Under Wilson E was a deposit of £400, Wow! Compare with his £6 a week as a builder's labourer.

'This has got to go to Forbesy tomorrow,' I insisted.

The following Monday morning, Smithy had been signed off and returned to the nick in Glossop Street on light duties. He swanned into the canteen and leaned on the counter. 'Cup of tea and a bacon sarnie, please, Kathy.' She grinned and crowed, 'Smithy, me old love! Good ter see yer – and you've still got your head on!'

'I have, but I don't know if it's still working!'

Behind him there was a burst of clapping, cheering and good natured mickey-taking.

'Thanks for all your cards and well-wishing – and for the clap.' Someone sniggered. 'OK, I'll rephrase that for the mucky-minded – thank you for the *applause!*' And he sat down with a grizzled old desk-sergeant and two WPC's and bit joyfully into his bacon sarnie. I came over and joined them, 'The Inspector wants to see you straight away, PC Smith' I said in my most official manner.

The sergeant rolled his eyes, mock-exasperatedly, Smith you've only just come back and you're up before the Inspector!'

'That's me, Sarge, always in trouble!'

The girls giggled, 'Bet he wants to give you a bunch of flowers,' teased Helen. 'Yeah and a box of Black Magic,' giggled Natalie.

Smithy gave them an owl-like look. 'And if he does, you two aren't getting any!'

'What about your favourite desk sergeant?'

'Sorry, Sarge, that would be bribing a senior officer.' He finished the last crumbs of his bacon butty, swigged the last of his tea and stood up. 'It'll be my P45 waiting for me,' he gloomed, and swept out amid gales of laughter.

CHAPTER 7

When we got to Forbesy's office, it wasn't roses, chocolates or P45, but a very serious discussion about certain detectives and their fiscal status.

'As you know, you didn't give me carte blanche to approach the bank, and the acting bank manager expressly forbade me to look in his files – but an anonymous source came across something. Look at these,' showing the inspector certain notes of bank statements with underlining. I repeated, 'These came from an anonymous source, so they may not be used in evidence. I'm not a grass, and I would never let my dislike of these officers cloud my judgement, but, Sir, what do you think?'

'I think we need the Superintendent down here!' reaching for the phone. 'Sir, we have a grave problem!' Superintendent Stacy was a copper's copper; always readily available for his lads, and the occasional lass that the station got, but didn't suffer foolishness, dishonesty or laziness easily. But he raced everywhere like Billy Whizz in the Beano. He blew into Forbesy's office like a tornado. Smithy and I stood up, but impatiently waving us down again, his words shot out like machine-gun fire, 'What is this about, Inspector? And what are these two PC's doing here? Isn't Smith still on sick-leave'

'We have had an anonymous tip-off that three of our station have been getting unexplained deposits put in their bank accounts. The tip-off came to Smith.'

'I said - aren't you on sick-leave, Smith?' sternly enquired Forbesy.

'I am, Sir, but the tip-off came to me. I've had a lot of friends visit; Judo people, the church, friends down the town. But this person absolutely demanded anonymity; out of fear, I think.' He held out the pre-tattered, authentic-looking Xerox.

The Super scanned it hastily, then, 'Right, Forbes. Get those three up here!'

Smithy, from the safety of his protective bandages dared to say, 'If I may, Sir. I've had a lot of thinking time just lately, and I fear that there are wheels within wheels within wheels with this one.'

'Explain!'

'Being off sick, and being well-visited, I hear all sorts. And there seems to be a malaise in the town just lately.'

I butted in, 'One of my er- shall we say contacts; a bit of a low life himself, has been giving me the odd snippet. Were you aware, Sir, or Mr Forbes, that there is now a brothel in town? And my contact has been badly beaten and razored after talking to me.'

Smithy picked the paper up, 'May I? dare I? suggest, Sir, that we let these characters run free; given enough rope, they may lead to who is paying them, and for what?' I wondered at his temerity; a lowly PC to the station Superintendent. But that was Smithy, all humility and reasonableness, but like a velvet steamroller.

'I will be honest with you two – I hate the idea of rats in our wainscot. In fact, I am furious – even more so that the news has only just come to me. And I trust that you and Smith, Watson, are not just tattling – but I know that Forbes and I have had unprovable suspicions.'

'Sir, there's no way that Smith or I are grasses,' I riposted through gritted teeth. 'But there's something here not right. Stinks like last week's salmon.'

The Super nodded wisely, 'I agree, constable. See to it, Forbes!' and with that he hurricaned out.

Little Joe turned luxuriously over on the tatty settee and gazed at the skinny blonde beside him, 'Good to see yer again, Daf. Missed yer.'

''Ere yer roughneck. I've got somethin' for yer.' Rummaging in her handbag.

Little Joe grinned salaciously. 'I know!'

'Somethin' else you blasted tomcat. Someone down the Smoke feels sorry for yer bein' chased, so they've sent yer some bread'n'honey. Two hundred an' fifty smackeroos.'

'Why?' suspiciously.

'There's just a little job that occasionally comes up. This kindly old man would just like you to offload some hot ciggies – maybe a bit o' heroin now an' again. it'll come in along the sands at Morecombe, and all you have to do is leave it in a certain place for it to be picked up. There's a ton in it every trip. An' the kind old man wants you to get hold of an old banger. And quick – the first lot is coming in next Monday.'

'This isn't the Sheldons, is it?' Joe shuddered.

'Think they'd bankroll you after chasing yer out?' she lied, 'No, my friend appreciates your business skills – as well as thinkin' you got a raw deal.'

Little Joe preened. It was good someone appreciated his business brain. 'Those idiot Sheldons, all brawn and no brain. Just bullies with too much money. Reckon I'd 'a' seen 'em off if I'd stayed down there!' he crowed.

Daf tried to look adoringly at Joe while thinking what a grade A halfwit he was. if every customer was as gullible as Joe, she could have retired years ago.

Joe turned on the radio, then grabbed her and threw her on the bed, whilst Tommy Steele complaining that he never felt more like singing the blues disguised the creaky old bed-noises.

Lord Lucas placed a bet on the 2:30 at Epsom, poured himself a refreshing lager, then re-dialled. 'Wilson? Are you settled in? bit of luck for you that the old Jap copped it!'

'Indeed, Sir! He was too old, too Japanese, too set in his ways and the club never went anywhere. All about keeping the scallies of the street, and making them honest. I intend to go all out for the Nationals – maybe one or two may even make international standard.'

Patronisingly, 'Very good Wilson. Keep it up, good chap. But what about our last little endeavour?'

'That's become a mess. The busies are around all the time. They haven't got anywhere, but they are all the time underfoot. One of Akeni's little bright boys has been questioning me about the club. I've had to warn him off.'

'Your problem, old man. My problem is that the last little endeavour didn't yield nearly enough. And I need seed-money.'

'I think I should lie low. Concentrate on the judo.'

'And I think you should get planning another expedition.'

'What if I refuse?'

'You'll be shopped. And the good thing about being a Peer of the Realm is that everybody will believe me, not you. *So get on with it!*'

Grumpily, Wilson agreed and started thinking where a next expedition should be; there were plenty of places round about that would bring a good yield. He thought maybe a raid on a store in Blackpool, this time of the year there were a lot of sweaty holiday makers spending like mad. Perhaps His High-and-Mightiness might bankroll a raid on one. *Have to do a bit of research down there,'* he thought to himself, *and I think I may have neutralised that couple of coppers, one of 'em still recovering from that crack on the head I gave him, another bleeding heart commie, all helping the community with his local wives and kids self-defence. Why can't the community help itself? And the big ugly one too thick to notice what's going on. Poncing up and down the High Street with his thumbs in his belt. Showing off to the shop girls. Get him on the mat and I'd show him.'*

In the evening we met at Amelia's, with the brain-lubrication of a chocolate sponge and a rather nice wine of some sort. I'm a beer-man myself, but it was rather nice. Smithy had an orange juice. I told Amelia about the meeting we'd had with Forbes and the Super, and suggested that we kept a low profile, but kept a low-level eye on our three bent coppers and the new brothel.

Little Joe strolled possessively to his new business venture above the chip shop. It had been a find – well-kept three-bed flat with a discreet door of its own round the back. He had decorated it in lush pinks and soft settees, with four-posters in the bedrooms, the special one with a mirror above the canopy. Then he waited for a cold, rainy night and drove the old Austin A40 into Blackpool. He cruised down the Golden Mile until he saw three bedraggled, skinny young ladies almost-dressed in very short skirts and skinny tops shuddering miserably in a doorway. He parked illegally and got out. As he approached them, they pathetically tried to look sexy, 'Evenin' Sailor, what can we do for yez?' asked the tall redhead in a broad Scouse accent.

'Not much going on tonight, Ladies,' sympathetically smiled Joe.

'Wotcher after? Impatiently asked the suicide blonde. The small elfin dark one just looked.

'I've got a proposition for you – a business proposition!' he added hastily. 'I've just moved up here from the Smoke to set up a new business. Not thirty miles from here I've got a drum that need some business partners. It's right in hayseed land, but you'd work from the flat – no going out on a night like this, and the locals are a bit earthy but clean. Want to come and have a look?'

The girls looked askance at each other, and whispered; 'We might miss a John!' 'It's cold out here.' 'What if he's a wierdo?' 'There's three of us.'

Joe gave a cosmopolitan sneer, 'Please yourselves, there's plenty of you lot around in holiday season. Up to you. But there's a pony each in it just for looking.'

So Joe started his new business venture with almost-blonde Joleen, diminutive Mary-Lou and redheaded Sharon. A discreet word round the pubs gave Joe a base of farm-workers, shop-boys and the bone-idle layabouts. But a 10% agent's fee on two pounds ten shillings didn't get Joe rich, so when established he trained the girls to carol pleasedtomeetcha and drink tea with their little fingers stuck out. And he put a discreet word round the golf-club and the Masonic Hall, and attracted a much better – and richer – class of client. 10% of fifty pounds a trick sounded much better. And the girls loved being sympathetic to the local posh lot whose twin-setted, pouter pigeon wives didn't understand them. There were local businessmen, gentlemen farmers – and policemen. And it wasn't long before his benefactor in London asked for names and addresses via Daffy.

The Sheldons plonked down on his white Harrods settee without asking. Lucas silently gritted his teeth, but said nothing. These plebs were still useful.

'Here, y'are yer lordship,' mocked Richard, 'Names, rank an' numbers as requested!' Richard had done his National Service in the Greenjackets. Mostly in the glasshouse.

Lucas stood up and took out his wallet, 'I think fifty pounds should cover it.'

'Not so fast, yer Lordliness,' said Rupert quietly, 'You did mean fifty each?' Lucas spluttered and got all patronising, but that bounced off; he was only a peer of the realm; they were kings of the East End. He needed them, so he capitulated, thinking gleefully of the day when they would really get their pay. His building firm used quite a lot of concrete in foundations.

CHAPTER 8

Farmer George Gregory called his Number One, Jeff Braddon, into his office, situated upstairs in his rather seedy nightclub.

He was called Farmer George because he wore country tweeds and a battered trilby hat. He had a round, rubicund face, kept country-fresh-looking with alcohol, affected what he thought was a woolly-back accent and smoked a disgusting old briar pipe. Strange, because he had never been near a farm, considering that anywhere out of the city was full of stinking animals, not all of which had four legs. He had been born in Liverpool Eight, had done his war-service safe in a communications bunker in Brighton, and had moved up to London to make his fortune. And make his fortune he did, specialising in brothels both high-class and low, and importing heroin for the upper-classes at play. He also ran what was ostensibly a boxing club, but in fact it hired out bouncers and minders of the less-gentle sort. He also promoted illegal bare-knuckle fights. He managed to get away with it because he had friends in Scotland Yard, and they knew he kept order in the underworld. He had a kindly eye and a sympathetic manner. Yet he was a cold-hearted a villain as you could never wish to meet. He was suspected of complicity in a number of discreet disappearances.

'Jeff, me old boy,' he drawled, 'I'm going away.'

'For very long?'

'For ever.'

'Why?'

'I've heard from that three-timing cow Daphne Doors that the Sheldons are after me – got a contract out. And I can't be bothered to fight – too old, too tired, and I've made all the bread-and-honey I'll ever need. So I'm off.'

'Spain?'

'Too many scallies already there, and too much Sheldon influence. No, Brazil. Maybe me and Hitler can get together!' he joked. 'But if I don't it may come to me or the Sheldons propping up a block of flats. And I can no longer be bothered. I'm sixty now; need new crumpet and a change of scene.'

'If you like, I'll take a bunch of the lads round and really sort them. Don't know who they think they are – especially that great mary-ellen, Rupert.'

Jeff was five-feet-eight of solid muscle and sinew, with massive shoulders and shovel hands, and a broken nose, memento of many a bare-knuckle fight or run-in down an alley. And the ethical sense of a hyperactive sewer rat.

'No, I'm going. But I'm giving you the boxing club. The Sheldons aren't after them – they only want this club and its toms, and, of course, the powder. But do me a favour. Remember that dirt-bag Wilson? Well, he double-crossed me. He was manager here long before your time and he sold me out. First to a team down Paddington way, then when they disappeared under a council-house, the Sheldons picked him up before I could get at him and packed him off to some thicko hayseed town up North, near Blackpool. He's running a judo club up there. And I want you to find as many ways as possible to make his life a misery. But don't kill him – I want him to suffer! I've said bye-bye to the lads with a grand each and here are the club deeds and three grand. You've been a good loyal manager and enforcer.' Giving a manly handshake he dismissed him.

Whistling cheerfully, he put on his old Barbour jacket and disreputable Trilby, went downstairs and locked up the club. 'Surprise! Surprise!' a voice hissed. There were six heavy shouldered hooligans, some with pickaxe-handles and at least one had a knife. They surrounded him and ushered him towards an idling J2 van.

George was no coward. He broke one's nose, rearranged another's testicles and gave another a solar plexus punch that left him gasping, but then the world went black.

Rupert Sheldon met Jeff in The Golden Hind; a sleazy spit-n-sawdust dive that belied its name.

'When done, Jeff, moi ould maate!' he mimicked. 'Any problems?'

'No, got on to you as soon as he shut the door. Never suspected a thing. Now…George gave me the deeds – and I reckon they're worth money… the going rate is about fifty thousand.'

'Not my going rate. I'll give you twenty. Plus a thousand for your trouble.'

'Not enough, Rupe. It's worth far more than that. Be reasonable.'

'Two things, Jeff, me old mucker.' Leaning forward and staring into Steve's eyes, 'Firstly, No-One-Ever-Calls-Me-Rupe. Ever. Not even my own grandma. So it's Mr Sheldon to you. Secondly, twenty grand is very reasonable. I could get it for free - off you still warm body. I have little respect for a guy who can sell out a boss who trusted him. I call such people sewer rats. And they live in cellars!'

Jeff understood perfectly. Tales of the Sheldon's cellar were rife. He gulped.

'OK Mr Sheldon,' he stammered, 'Fair offer.'

Rupert clicked his fingers and a broad-shouldered, blue-chinned vassal materialised at his shoulder with an attache case. Opening it, Rupert carelessly tossed bundles of fivers on the bar. 'Twenty-one grand. Don't bother counting it – I'm not dishonest!' He chuckled at his own joke. 'Now, I've got a little job for you. It's up near Blackpool. Remember Little Joe?'

Steve gulped again. Rumour was that Little Joe was swimming along the bottom of the Thames. Rupert smiled. 'No, Joe's not dead. Next best thing. Living in Blackpool.' Again Rupert smiled at his own wit. 'I have a client in import/export, based in Morecambe. On the beach. Things – and people – come in. things – and people go out. I've set Joe up in a brothel, and he organises things. With the help of a lady called Daphne Doors. But he's no enforcer – far too soft. So I need a hard case up there. Not all the local hayseeds and cotton-weavers appreciate a little competition. You're appointed.' Jeff nodded. Hard case or not, you always agreed with the Sheldons. 'You'll have a retainer of £15 a week, and a bonus of £50 every time a shipment goes through OK. And a slapping if it doesn't. Fair do's, Steve?'

'Very fair, Mr Sheldon.'

Inspector Forbes called me into his office. 'This comes down from the Super, Bill. And it's not for publication. HQ in Hutton have had a whisper. A brothel has opened up on our patch and we need to get rid of it. We're not sure where it is, so keep your eyes open for any of the local bachelors or hen-pecked husbands with smiles on their faces.'

Remembering I'd already told him, I nodded then smiled and fingered my truncheon. 'No, not like that, Watson, you hooligan. Legally. You hear me? Legally.'

'OK if I clue Smithy in, Sir?'

'Yes, and Mrs Giles. But no one else – especially not in the station. Now go!'

I right wheeled and marched smartly out, regulation boots clattering on the floor. As I passed the CID desk, Johnson leered at me. 'Been wound the inspectwor, Biwwy-boy?'

I looked at him consideringly, then stepped forward. His eyes sharpened with nerves. I reached forward and planted a kiss on his scrofulous scalp, and twisted his spare tyre. Not gently. I smiled. 'That'th from your best fwiend!' I minced. The room laughed. Johnson growled.

Time passed. The seasons rolled round. And after a whole year, Smithy was pulling at his lead to get off light duties and be considered as fit to resume outdoor service. But still light duties until the specialist says OK. We had wracked our brains for Sensei's murder. With Amelia we had brainstormed, what-iffed and eaten Amelia's home baking. But got nowhere. However, I had located the brothel – above the chip-shop, and had begun standing very conspicuously outside at pub throwing-out time Fridays and Saturdays and Sunday lunchtimes. Strange, but parking seemed a lot better recently. And I had my ears out with my snouts.

Richard bounced into Grandma's kitchen, slapped Rupert on the back, grabbed a beer from the new-fangled fridge, slumped onto a hard kitchen chair and spoke. 'Rupert, dear bro, we have a problem. You know we set Little Joe up with a knocking-shop? There's been a nosy copper putting the mockers on trade. We need him out.'

'Send a couple of the lads up?'

'No – we have to be subtle. Duff up a copper in one of those dead-end woolly-back towns, and you won't see the place for bluebottles. Subtle my boy, subtle! We send Daffy up there – she'll shake him out of his tunic.'

'And trousers!' Rupert gloated.

Smithy continued digging into Sensei's murder and the bank robbery. He had not a shred of a lead, not a whisper, but he thought it too coincidental that both his cracked skull and Sensei's murder had happened at the judo club.

And then there was Wilson appearing and taking over the club. He had not been part of that club, and Sensei would not have tolerated the bullyragging and violence that Wilson taught; it was the very opposite of the ethos of Judo, 'the Gentle Way.' Smithy – unlike me – always had a tendency, due to his faith, I guess, to make allowances, even to the no-goods, but he admitted that Wilson was giving him an itch he couldn't scratch.

He spent hours on the phone with his Judo Conference directory, talking to fellow judoka, especially coppers, who may know anything at all about Wilson.

Eventually he dug up George Moore, whom he knew quite well, a recently retired but still whipcord-fit ex detective sergeant; sixth dan who attended a club in Harrow. He knew Wilson very well, having busted him on numerous occasions. 'So, young Smith, what's your beef with Wilson? What's the useless waste of time, thought and energy been up to up there in yokel-land?'

'Well, yer honour, oi do be a-thinking he be up to something with moi old club.'

'A frustrating case, is Wilson. He had potential. He was a fast learner and achieved dan-grade in no time. But as he got up the grades, he got more and more violent – he had to win at all costs. He got his club membership taken off him just after he made fifth dan. He almost crippled a fellow club member.

'Now his criminal record. How long's your arm? I've busted him a number of times, brawling, protection, GBH. He worked as an enforcer and a club bouncer for a very nasty team, run by two brothers, the Sheldons. We finally got him when he was bribing who he thought was a bent copper. He got a year in Strangeways, up in Manchester. He got out last year and managed to con the Judo Council into accepting him as a reformed character.'

'He's not. He took over my old club after Sensei Ateni was murdered. He's run it in to the ground, so now it's just Thugs' Paradise. I think he's into criminal heavy stuff up here, as well.'

'Smithy, lad, I heard about your Sensei's murder, and understand how you want to get 'em, but aren't you too involved? Wouldn't it be better to leave it to your CID?'

'You've never met our scummy CID. Bone idle, and I wouldn't trust them as far as I could throw their overweight corpuses!'

'Do I detect a hint that you don't really like them? But be careful, Bulldog Drummond. You know station politics.'

'It's OK, I'm off on a long sick leave. Got bashed over the head with a nunchuka. Cracked skull.'

'Sorry to hear that, but it doesn't seem like it's let any sense in!'

'Thanks, pal! Anyway, this gen. is very useful. And of course you didn't tell me anything of this.'

'Anything of what?'

'Have a great retirement, mate. Bless you.' Smith put the phone down very thoughtfully.

Smithy kept on the research. The murder of the old Sensei Ateni had gone into the dead file bin for lack of evidence. But Smithy kept on.

Then a break came. I was walking around the lake in the town's park, and noticed a young woman seated in the porch of the redundant boathouse. She smiled. 'Evening, Officer.' Her voice was London but pleasant. She was smartly dressed, flower-print tunic top, tartan trews and flat heeled shoes. Respectable, but something said look out. Not an obvious tom like the ones in the chippy, but a look; something at the back of my mind said careful!

'Afternoon, Miss,' at my most plodworthy, 'can I help?'

'I wonder if you could, I've just moved up here to look after my granny.' (*Granny my foot!* I thought.) 'And I don't really know people. I'm too busy with Gran.'

'Is she ill?'

'Not really. Just old age. She's eighty-seven. Marvellous for her age, but…you know.'

I decided that I'd go along with the honey-trap. 'I could show you a few places nice enough for a respectable girl like you,' I mused.

'Oh, would you? I'd be ever so grateful! Gran's tucked up in bed and asleep by eight.'

'I could meet you here at eight,' I pondered, 'It's still light. We could have a stroll and end up in Sarah's Coffee Bar. That's the town's answer to the 2Is'

'Ooh! That would mean so **much** to me!' *Yes, a hundred quid*, she gloated to herself, *soon get this thick plod – what's the word? Comp…com – promised.* 'I'm Brenda."

'And I'm Arthur.' I touched my helmet, PC Dixon style and strolled on

When I told Amelia and Smithy they both chortled, 'Bill, you Beootiful lady-killer,' Amelia crooned. Smithy, pseudo-interested said, 'Find out if she's got a mate!'

The following evening I strolled into the park, dressed best cavalry twill trousers and sports jacket, and found Brenda waiting for me. I sat beside her. In the background Smithy and Amelia walked a borrowed dog up and down.

'I'm so glad you made it, Arthur! I get so lonely. People are friendly enough, but I can't understand the lingo!'

'Eyup, Lass, tha's talkin' to one!' She smiled an answer.

As we started to rise, Smithy eeled forward, pointing at the top of her jeans, 'Are you carrying, or is that a bad hernia?'

She reached reflexively for the gun, but Amelia's steely grip held her. 'I really wouldn't, young lady!' in a voice that had quelled classroom riots, 'Sit!'

I held out my warrant-card. Smithy held out his. Amelia smiled in the background.

'I promised you a little walk, and so we shall,' I smiled, 'And if you're honest you might even get that coffee.'

I held her hand, lover-like but firm, and Smithy and Amelia followed closely behind. We came to the edge of Quarry Wood. Her eyes widened in fear. She whimpered.

'Don't worry, sweetheart, we're Lancashire Police, not KGB or Gestapo. But we do need answers. And carrying a concealed weapon in this town could send you hurtling back to London – to a five-stretch in Holloway. Good looking lass – the girls will love you.' We sat on a bench in the gathering dusk. Amelia's kind but irresistible voice began, 'Now, young lady, real name, please.'

'Daphne Doors.' She looked at us; suspicious, fearful; a hardness about her that was unwilling to believe that nothing bad was going to happen – because it always had.

'Now, please the *real* real name.'

'Maisie Billings.' Sulkily.

'So what' going on?'

'I daren't!' Shivering.

'You daren't what?'

'They'll kill me!'

'Who'll kill you? Listen, Maise, you have two choices. If you tell me honestly – and I'll know if you're lying - we can get you out from under, and send you far out of reach. But if you stay stumm or lie, it's that five-stretch and the we'll make sure the prisoners will know all about you.'

Eventually, she cracked. In floods of tears she told us. She had been brought up poor but solid working class, mother worked in a shop, father was a milkman. She was never gorgeous, but the men seemed to like her, she said. A rich man much older than her had fancied her and said he'd take her to a concert. Her mum had bought her a new dress and some cheap earrings and she had been picked up in a new Jaguar Mark Seven.

'But instead of going to a concert,' she said bitterly, 'I was driven to a wood in Essex, given some sort of firewater to drink - and raped – again and again. My new dress was in shreds. I was kicked out of the car outside my home and when my mother saw the state I was in she refused to believe me, packed a suitcase and threw me out. Then,' she continued, 'round the corner was a new Jaguar Mark Seven. "Get in, I knew this would happen – it always does – and you're mine now." He put me on the streets and I became what you see!' she sobbed even louder.

Her orders were to walk me to somewhere quiet but still near people, wave the gun, which wasn't loaded, make me take my trousers off, then she'd scream rape. 'And the gun wasn't even loaded anyway,' she gloomed.

"Why? Who's that interested in a mere small-town plod?"

"There's a team down the East End, very well-connected, very dangerous. They're moving up here. They own the local brothel. They want to move into Blackpool and Morecombe. And they want you out of it and in their pockets, Arthur,"

"Bill!"

"Bill then, you were losing them money, sniffing round all the time."

"Who are these mobsters? The guy running it seems to be a bit pathetic."

"He's little Joe.he lives in a world of his own, but he's very timid. They're the Sheldon Brothers. Psychopaths, murderers, drugs, girls – not just pro's like me; some get sent abroad – not always willingly. They terrify me! And they chased Joe up here to expand their business. He doesn't know it – he thinks he's boss. But I come up every month to make sure he's behaving himself – and give him a bit of – er – encouragement."

"Right," said Amelia, "Strongly suggest, Bill, you report this to the Inspector, and if he agrees, I can get Maise – Daphne – Brenda to a girls' home run by nuns, very kind; very helpful and understanding. But sharp. And if you run or try to, these two lads here will throw the book at you. And shop you to these Sheldons. Eventually they will need you as a witness. Now, Bill and Smithy, can we officially say the gun was not loaded; a bit of horseplay, and not press charges?"

Smithy gave Maisie the Smithy eyeball, cool, remote, implacable. "If the Inspector and Super agrees, we'll let it go. But if not, you're busted. And if you try it on, you're busted. And if you go back to prostitution, you're busted."

"But you don't know the Sheldons. They really are psychopaths. They're strong, violent, and stop at nothing. They're absolutely terrifying. They are very pleasant to me. But you know that kid's song, Never Smile at a Crocodile? That's how I feel when I'm with them. They use me to keep Joe and others in line. They don't just kill, they torture first. Then it's propping up a tower block for you. I don't know why I'm telling you this. They'll get me!"

Smithy asked, now very gentle and understanding, "Do they have anything else going up here? I used to belong to the local judo club, and my sensei – my teacher, guide and friend was murdered during a bank-robbery and I want to know why."

"Dunno, but there is some guy up here runs a some sort of club for that stuff. Called Wilson. Had to come up here because his violence got him noticed down the Smoke."

I glanced at Smithy. He was thinking, and if I know Smithy he'd be praying as well.

Then Amelia spoke. "My friend – she's a nun – a girl I taught – runs a home for all sorts of girls under distress; pregnant teenagers kicked out, reforming prostitutes, battered wives, junkies and alkies trying to get clean…she's not soft, not by any means, but she's understanding and loving. She's Ruth Sharpe, but now Sister Marie Clare. If you seriously want out, and will get stuck in to a hard but healthy life, she's your girl. it's about as far from the East End as you can get. It's right up in the Western Highlands, near Acharachle. It's near where the Commandos trained. No way these brutes will get you up there."

"Oh, could you? Would you? I'm scared to go back to London a failure. I'll do anything!"

Smithy emerged from his prayer trance. "So you need to disappear. Tonight. No trace of you to be found. Do you have a cheque-book?"

"Who, me? Not on your nelly. I get cash when I need it from my POSB."

"Good. No problem there then. But we need to create a legend to get you up there and leave no trace of you here. I don't believe in lying but if it's your safety, I will, and apologise to God later. So how about this. There is a local produce merchant that I know who delivers all over the country, including up in the Highlands about once a week. I think it's tomorrow. You're Helen and you're too scared to give your last name. You need to get away from a wife-battering husband who has clout locally. The driver is trustworthy and can keep his mouth shut. He's a member of the church I go to, so there'll be no funny business of any sort. We'll get him to pick you up way down the road, no connection with here. But you must be straight – no messing about, no lies, no con-game. Bill, Amelia and I want to help you, but we're not softies. Say now, can we trust you? Do we send you? Yes or no."

She broke down. "Oh yes! I can't do this anymore! Please!"

Amelia muttered to us, "I know when girls are trying it on. And this one isn't. We'll send her. But for your own safety, Maisie, no phone calls, no letters. You must be just plain gone. I will stay in touch with Sister Marie Clare, to make sure you're all right."

We walked back into town. Smithy disappeared into a phone box, and came out beaming. "My buddy is making a pickup in Chorley at five am tomorrow. he'll pick you up there. Then straight up to Scotland. Amelia, would you mind driving us? we'll sleep in the car, and as of now you cease to exist as Daphne. Why Daphne Doors, anyway?"

"Rupert Sheldon, who doesn't like girls gave me that name, like Diana Dors the actress." I smirked, anyone less like the voluptuous blonde Miss Dors was hard to imagine. Maisie glared.

Maisie was still sobbing; gut-wrenching sobs coming up from deep inside, nose running into Amelia's handkerchief and eye makeup leaving black snail-trails all down her face. "Why are you doing this for me? A stranger? I've had a life on the game since I was thirteen; all those dirty old paederasts always said, "no time to be superstitious!" like they were being clever and I'd never heard it before. I had trouble not throwing up. And today I set out to hurt you, Bill, to stitch you up and finish you as a copper. Why this now?"

Smithy, lasers gentle, gazed at her. "Because under all that, whatever you've done; whatever's been done to you, you are a unique human being, who needs a chance. And God loves you."

"He can't, not a slimeball like me!"

"Well, strangely enough he does. And here's a chance to let him prove it."

"Yes," Amelia said, "And you'll find Marie Clare won't push religion down your throat. You can attend services in the chapel if you want, but you're not forced to. She'll just love God at you.

CHAPTER 9

Maisie thanked Bernard the driver and, slipping three one pound notes on the dash, emerged stiff and sore outside the pub in Acharachle. 'It's raining!' she groaned.

'This is Scotland, Luv,' Bernard said, 'It's always raining. Tara, Luv and God bless.' Maisie was overawed. As a Cockney born-and-bred the hills, the emptiness and the silence completely spun her head over.

Across the road was a ramshackle ex-army Land Rover with two grinning faces by it. neither looked like nuns. They strolled over. 'Maisie-called-Daphne-called-Helen we presume. Mrs Sykes, my old teacher rang ahead. I'm Marie Clare, and this is Abigail Frances.'

Maisie was gobsmacked. She was expecting little old ladies in long black gowns and tall wimples with severe expressions. Marie Clare was tall, statuesque and very blonde. And by the way she manhandled Maisie's rucksack into the back of the Landie, strong as well. Abigail Frances was small and buxom, and very black. Both were dressed in 'civvies,' both were about thirty. Abigail was dressed in tartan trews and grey anorak, Marie Clare hiking trousers and blue anorak. Both wore big boots.

'Close yo mouth, Girl!' smiled Abigail in a chocolate-soft Caribbean accent, 'We're the plain-clothes branch. But seriously, we're of a missionary order, and our calling is to share God's love with everyone.'

'Yes!' grinned Marie Clare, 'we have a special dispensation to wear civvies; dressing like real people helps everyone - including you, I hope – to accept us as real people.' Her accent was very much the correct English of the Dublin Pale.

'But make no mistake, we are both 'married' to God, and here we are to love and serve Him. But we do have fun!' a great beaming grin split Abigail's cute little face in half.

Over the weeks Maisie settled into the Spartan life in the St Teresa's farm. It was hard work, feeding free range hens and geese and looking for eggs, hoeing weedy crops, spud-picking, and cutting cabbages. At first she went to bed in her little cell, aching and worn out and collapsed unconscious. But gradually she grew muscles in places that she never knew she had places, and the pure Highland air made her lungs work as never before. And she got to know the other girls' stories and found she wasn't unique. After an initial suspicion she accepted their help and kindness. And got to know the other nuns. After a while she started to attend the twice-daily services, basking in a peace and serenity she had never known. Gradually the words began to make sense. And she began to be useful in getting alongside the other girls; comforting them when they woke up sobbing or screaming. And she was always ready to do more than her fair share of gardening or housework.

Then on a quite ordinary Monday morning, as she lay awake ready for the six o'clock bell for Matins. An overpowering thought hit her, blinded her and broke her. 'You are my child,' the thought thundered round her head, 'You have learned to trust me. I am with you all the time. Now I want you. I want you here. As a nun'"

She told the thought, 'you don't know me. I think you're God. Or am I going mad? You're pure. I'm not. You can't want me! After all the bad stuff I've done! Tomming, selling Joe down the river! Trying to stitch up Bill! You can't trust me! But who are you? Are you real or just me cracking up?'

'I AM who I Am. And I know you better than you know you., and I do want you. I trust you. I was with you when you daren't go home from school in case your 'uncle' was there. I was with you when you trembled with cold on a street corner. When you trembled with fear at the Sheldons. And when you trembled with dawning belief here. **I WANT YOU!** I want you so I can love you. I want to love others through you. I want you as a nun.' She felt the weight of the past slip off. She felt a warm glow inside. She wept.

Then, jumping out of her hard, narrow bed ran into Marie Claire's cell. 'Marie! Marie Clare!' Marie Claire dragged herself out of the depths, and off her simple plank bed. 'Huh?' she asked intelligently, 'Tha' you, Maisie?'

'Marie Clare! I want to be a nun!'

Snapping awake, Marie Clare grinned in disbelief; mouth open. 'You do? Am I awake?'

Maisie nodded.'

'How I've prayed for this!' and leaping out of bed hugged Maisie so tightly her ribs creaked. 'Straight after breakfast, we'll talk! Blessyou, blessyou, blessyou!' she ran into Abigail's cell, 'Abby! Abby! Wake up!'

A drowsy head surfaced from beneath the single grey blanket. 'Whattonearthyou screaminabout-girl?'

'It's me, Abby! Maisie! God spoke to me! He says he loves me! I can't believe it! an' I wanna be a nun! I wanna be like you an' Marie Clare!"

'WHAAAT? screamed Abigail. 'I've prayed for you since you got here! You were such a pathetic little drowned rat! Now look at you!' Jumping out of bed, she danced round the room, whirling Maisie till she was dizzy. The noise woke the other nuns and the girls, and they too danced round the cell – even Sister Martha, who was ninety and very arthritic.

Marie Clare and Abigail quizzed her unmercifully. One of the other nuns, overhearing, said, 'You two should remuster to the KGB – they'd welcome you. Give the poor girl a chance!' But after two days of grilling, the two sisters stood up in Vespers and said 'Please welcome our new postulant, Maisie! She will be leaving us soon for four weeks in a nunnery near Perth, then she will be accepted as a novice. We'll all go and see her take her vows. Then she will have a new name; Sister Virginia, after a sixteenth century nun who was made a saint for her helping poor people and being a peacemaker.' An explosion of clapping, whistling, shouting., 'Good on yer, girl!' 'Go for it. Maze!'

'When the noise dies down, we'll send you down to Glasgow to our mother house, to *get done* properly.'

CHAPTER 10

Smithy had a talk booked to give to the fifth and sixth years of the local Grammar School on self-defence and keeping safe. I went along to be literally the fall-guy.

When we walked in, dressed in civvies; grey flannel trousers open necked shirts and sports jackets there was an expectant buzz. The school was agog. Smithy was a legend having arrested four very drunk, very violent Scousers running amok in a local pub single handed. And they all felt sorry for him, still in his medical turban. And I was known as the beat-bobby in the school's area. We were greeted with a rousing cheer.

The Head gestured for silence, then introduced us as PC Smith and PC Watson. After the head had asked Smithy about his recovery, he handed over to us. Smithy started straight in. 'A bit different to usual, today; we're going to start with questions. There's so much esoteric rubbish talked about self-defence and Martial Arts, that I want to be quite clear.'

'Sir?' from a weedy bespectacled fifth-year boy, 'Will a self-defence course stop me from being bullied?'

There were a few jeers from the back of the hall. I strolled over, smiled benevolently at a bunch of lounging insolent lads and gently inquired, loud enough for everyone to hear, 'Any of you warriors care to let Smithy demonstrate?' Silence.

'What's your name, lad?' Smithy asked, 'Frank? Self-defence is not a magic wand, it won't turn you into Charles Atlas or Rocky Marciano; that takes years of rigorous training. But get on a self-defence course, get to a boxing club or a Judo club – don't go near the local one - and you will get a confidence that bullies will steer clear of.'

'But what if the bullies do a self-defence course as well?' From a bright-looking Upper sixth girl. She smiled ruefully, as though she too had been bullied.

'Very few bullies are not cowards. They have to pick on the weak to convince themselves that they are strong – at least they try to think so. So don't be weak. Ven if you are feeling overpowered, don't show it."

Some of the questions were a bit daft; 'Why aren't you in your judo suits?'

'This is defence for real life. When did you last see anyone walking down the main street in a gi and mat-slippers?'

After a few more questions, Smithy got right in. 'President Roosevelt said, "Walk softly, but carry a big stick." That is good advice for a quiet life. Don't go looking for trouble. Self-defence is not just a fighting-skill; it's an attitude. So, lads, curb the testosterone, don't "come the hard case," there's always someone out there harder. And girls, lose any attitude of being the weaker sex. You're not. Walk softly, but carry a big stick.'

'Now, a few do's and don'ts. Rule One, be sensible. Girls in particular, when you go out, try to stay in a group; don't walk off with a guy you don't know. And not too many under-age Babychams.' (Tutting from certain aged staff members.) Lads, try not to provoke or be provoked. The best way of fighting is not fighting. I've taken too many young guys and girls up to the County Hospital who didn't follow these simple rules. And I've sat with too many shattered parents.'

A buzz of disappointment rambled round the room. That was tame!

'That's the boring but essential bit out of the way,' Smithy continued, 'so, just before Bill and I demonstrate, remember – Confidence! Confidence! Confidence! Most violence on the streets, or mugging, or rape isn't really about sex or money; (More tuts from the older lady teachers) it's about power; power over you. Try to walk away; don't run, it raises the hunting instinct, and don't plead. Don't argue; you argue, they have got you into their dialogue; you're dancing to their tune. You need to convince them that you're in charge - you're a winner and you're not scared of them – even if you are. They don't like losing. They may walk away, grumbling and threatening. But it doesn't always work. So before we teach you a few basic get-out-of-trouble tricks let's learn how to not get into trouble; girls, Victorian ladies carried hatpins to give unwanted suitors a quick jab. Dare

I suggest a pair of drawing-compasses fit the modern bill? Or a hairspray across the eyes. It will temporarily blind and sting, but no lasting damage. We're not about crippling anyone. And lads if you are cornered, pennies in the fist, or a metal watch strap make good knuckle dusters.

"Finally, and of utmost importance – self-defence is *defence!* If Bill or I hear of anyone using the techniques we teach as aggression or to settle an argument, you will be down to the police station before you can say ouch! And we won't go soft on you!'

Then Smithy and I demonstrated what to do if attacked from front or rear, how to block or avoid punches and how to get out of strangles. 'Now', Smithy said, "you've seen the demo; find a partner of about your size and practice!'

The hall was filled with bumps and giggles as they practiced.

Then, after a formal thank you and an immense cheer from the kids, the Head approached us with a little brown envelope – expenses.

'sorry, Sir,' at my most policemanly, 'We can't accept. So please put it in your school funds to take the kids out somewhere.'

'It was my staff who persuaded me to invite you, especially my recently-retired Head of English, Amelia Giles, but why do you as policemen see this sort of thing as necessary? Isn't it making the violence worse?'

'The concept and the hope is that kids – and adults – who are taught self-defence properly are less likely to promote trouble, and are more able to escape injury if attacked.'

'these young people,' I picked up, 'are growing up in an increasingly violent society. Our intention is to train them to avoid that violence – and the fear of it.'

Thoughtfully shaking hands, the Head wished us good luck. And we left.

Outside, Amelia was leaning against her car chatting to some of her old pupils. As they said goodbye and wished her a happy retirement, she asked one striking looking Caribbean girl to stay back. 'Bill! Smithy! Over here!' she called. 'Cynthia here has something to tell you.'

Lowering her eyes, a Caribbean sign of respect, Cynthia began in a honey-soft accent, 'Well, Sirs, you know the er...the er...that place above the chip shop,' a blush suffused her face darkly, 'well, there's a new girl works with me as a Saturday cleaner in the chip shop there, and over in a…er…a place in Blackpool, she's black like me. And she's a…well…more than a cleaner in Blackpool. We got talking in the local café. My mum and dad would have a fit if they knew I was talking to her. But she's lonely and she hates what she's having to do, watching disgusting old men putting their 'Cynthia blushed even more and stopped, hand to mouth. 'Sorry Sirs, Miss …I got a bit carried away.' Blushing again, 'She came over here with her parents for a better life but ended up homeless and despised. Terrible for us trying to get a home; "no dogs, no blacks, no Irish." She's disabled, has to walk on two crutches. Couldn't get a job; female, black and crippled. Some of the perverts like that sort of thing.' Cynthia's mouth turned down bitterly. 'I want to be a dentist. I'm near the top of this school. But I'm black and a girl!' Then she smiled reminiscently, 'but the lad in my class who called me a nignog still has to drink through a straw!' Then she picked up her story, 'A…er…you know…one of those people picked her up. Could use as a *prostitute* she whispered use her, but gave her a job cleaning here as well. But she's nosy, can't resist listening at doors. And she's heard something about smuggling across Morecombe sands – she thinks both people and drugs. But she's not sure what dates this happens.'

'Cynthia, you've done a great job here, drug-dealers kill people with their noxious stuff, and the people smuggled are often Vietnamese trying to get away from the rebellion against the French. They end up as slaves – or in a house like your friend mentioned. Would she meet us?'

Amelia cut in, 'if she will, best she meets just me, Cynthia knows me and I'm a woman. She will not like men at all.'

A week later, Amelia bustled into Smithy's digs. 'Cynthia rang - her mate, Ade - rang her today! There's a trawler due to land contraband on Morecombe Beach Sunday night!'

CHAPTER 11

Sunday. Midnight. The rusty, wheezy old trawler chugged to a halt just inside the three mile limit. A dilapidated net crane crankily lowered the exhausted wreck of a DUKW on to the surface of the sea. Then a group of apprehensive people were chivvied down a climbing net into it. And a different load of white paper sacks were put in. the DUKW reluctantly started, blew clouds of blue smoke and chugged shorewards. The water was rough. Some of the immigrants were seasick and got cursed by the smugglers. At last they landed.

And a dazzle of searchlights lit up the scene. Immigrants and sailors ran every way, to be caught by enthusiastic policemen. I jumped out of the van, bellowing, 'Stay there!' to Smithy. Who totally ignored me, running across the sand shouting, 'Bill! The DUKW!'

The DUKW had started up in a blue haze, and the ramp was beginning to jerk up. Smithy, head-bandage flying, jumped on board, followed by me. A sailor stood in Smithy's way, wielding a pipe-wrench. Ducking, Smithy *ogoshi-ed* him towards me. I laid him out with a punch on the point and nicked his pipe wrench. We continued to rush the driving seat. Two crew grabbed Smithy and punched him on his injured head. Stepping up behind, I cracked the pipe wrench across one's shoulder, then behind the knee. As he tried to get up I uppercut him. He slept; a sack of spuds. Smithy allowed the other to grab his arm, wound into him and *seoi-nage-ed* him six feet into the air. From which he sailed overboard and landed with a wet smack on the sand.

The driver turned round cursing and pulling an ex-army Webley automatic from his pocket. A crack from the pipe wrench dissuaded him by breaking his wrist. Smithy, being kind, promised not to handcuff his injured wrist, but fastened the good one to a stanchion. Then he turned round to grin, pitched forward, and collapsed, blood running out of his mouth. I grabbed my walkie-talkie and gabbled, 'Officer hurt, on DUKW. Ambulance needed! Pronto!'

Times like this I wished I had Smithy's faith – or anybody up there to talk to. Instead I just glared at him and snarled, 'Smith you great idiot! I told you to stay in the van! Who do you think you are? Superman? You go and die on me I'll never forgive you!' then, realising what I just said, gave a grin. Smithy's eyes opened, and he muttered, 'You're not getting rid of me that easily, Watson, you oaf.' His eyed rolled up and he went very flaccid.

Thankfully, an ambulance came racing across the sand, bell clanging frantically. In no time, Smithy was stretchered, cocooned and loaded into it and it sped off to Lancaster Royal Infirmary. I jumped in the nearest available police car and sped off. At the hospital I phoned Amelia, who immediately jumped into her 800cc Austin A30 and scorched up the A59 at a flat out 62mph. She arrived within the hour, and with her was the gorgeous nurse from Smithy's previous contretempts.

'Say hello to Alicia, Bill. She was worried so I grabbed her, told her Ward Sister she was needed for an emergency – and here she is!'

'Hi, Alicia, good to see you, if not in these circumstances. But where has that secretive ratbag been keeping you?'

She blushed and stuttered, 'Er…at church and…er…sometimes the coffee bar in Bradkirk.'

'Well, Girl, I admire his taste, if not his common sense in tackling baddies!'

Amelia ground out, schoolteacher glasses flashing, 'Just wait till he wakes up! He will certainly find the sharp edge of my tongue!' And promptly burst int tears. Alicia joined her. I didn't – I just passed my handkerchief.

It seemed like hours had passed when a stout bearded surgeon – James Robertson Justice to the tee – smiled and said, 'He's out of danger. You can go in to see him. But take a minute to tell me what he's been doing.'

'We were arresting a bunch of people-and-drug smugglers who had a DUKW,' I said nonchalantly. 'The DUKW tried to get away. Despite my distinct and specific instructions, that already-injured idiot in there ran and boarded her. And he hasn't even got over a broken skull yet!'

'I can see that! But unfortunately, he reopened the wound. He is very lucky to be alive.'

'When I've finished, he'll wish he was dead! I will certainly pound that fact into his head!" snarled Amelia. The surgeon took a step back. 'Mother?'

'Surrogate-mother-by-default,' grinned Amelia. 'Somebody's got to look after these two imbeciles,' nodding at me.

'Me too,' nodded Alicia.

We went into the ward. Smithy was awake. Alicia and Amelia hugged him tightly enough to burst his stitches.

Alicia and I returned down the long weary A59 to duty. Amelia stayed with him. Then I got a frantic phone call, 'Bill! Get up here! Someone's tried to murder Smithy!'

It transpired that Amelia had gone for a coffee and a comfort break, but when she returned, there was a balaclava-ed figure holding a pillow over Smithy's face. She had quickly picked up a full ceramic bedpan, thew the contents in its face and hit it on the head with the bedpan. It fled, staggering. 'So look for a very smelly criminal with a sore head!' she finished.

With Forbes' permission I nicked a police Wolsey 4/44 and cranked it all the way to Lancaster, just as the local plod arrived, in the shape of a cocky brand-new-and-shiny inspector. 'And who are you?' he barked at Amelia. In full pupil-quelling Lady Windermere mode she rose up and said, 'Young Man!' reducing him to an inky-fingered schoolboy. 'I would consider it a courtesy and a kindness that you would *not* address me in that manner!' and sat down.

Discomfited, the inspector turned om me. 'And you are?'

'PC 102 Watson, Sir!' I replied stiffly.

'And what are you and PC Smith doing on my patch?'

I stood even more to attention, gazed over his right shoulder and said in best military manner, 'Arresting suspects connected with people and drug smuggling! Sir!' His countenance, brick red before turned bright purple. 'And why was I not informed?' he barked.

'Top Secret Home Office Business, Sir!'

'You expect me to believe that? Are you and…?'

'PC Smith, Sir!'

'Are you and Smith involved? Two PC's? You expect me to believe you?'

'No Sir, but I do expect you to believe my inspector and my superintendent!' handing him the ward telephone.

Our Super is a quiet man. But when he barks – you know you've been barked at. The inspector began pompously about two PC's, one damaged on his patch. Then he spluttered. Then he expostulated. Gradually, he turned from purple to white. His voice dropped many decibels, and he stood to attention. Amelia an I could hear the Super's roar. 'Two of my best men…one injured in the line, of duty…nothing to do with you or your station…top secret Red Folder…'

The inspector tried to break in.

'Of course I don't trust you or your men!' The Super retorted. 'How long has this been going on under your noses? Are you corrupt or incompetent?'

The inspector tried again.

'Of course, I'll be reporting you to the Chief constable. Harassing two policemen on duty, one lying gravely injured - and a civilian visitor! How long have you had your inspector's rank? I can't guarantee you'll have it long enough to get used to it! and, finally, *Inspector*…all this is under the Official Secrets Act. So your lips are sealed!' we heard him slam the phone down.

The inspector left without a word. We grinned at his retreating back.

CHAPTER 12

'Wilson here!' curtly.

'Wilson, my old mate, we have a problem – at least you have!'

'Who are you? Richard or Rupert?'

'It doesn't matter. Let me explain in words simple enough for a thicko who ran away to peasant-land to get.'

Wilson seethed, but it didn't do to cross the Sheldons, so he swallowed his pride, ungritted his teeth and asked, 'What problem?'

'You remember the delightful Maisie Biggins – Daphne Doors to you? I sent her up to your neck of the woods to seduce a copper? Well, she's disappeared. No sign of her. Never reported in. Gone! And your job is to find her. There's a ton in it if you find her...and a thumping if you don't.'

'You had remembered that I am a fifth-dan black belt?'

'And *you* had remembered that I have six heavies just waiting to cut somebody?'

Again Wilson swallowed, and grumpily replied, 'I'll see what I can do. Who's the copper?'

'Some thick plod called Watson. Been hanging around Little Joe's, scaring the punters. Sent Maisie to get into his round-the-houses. And she's gone – vanished! See to it! remember the choices!'

'I know him. A bit of a sea-green incorruptible. Fancies himself as a hard case. Big mates with another copper called Smith. Fancies himself as a bit of a judoka, always smarming round the women with a self-defence course. On sick leave. The back of his head attacked a nunchuka! It will be a pleasure and a privilege to smack these two around a bit.'

"Just...Find...Maisie!'

'Okay, Boss! I'm on it!'

The phone rang. "Yeh? Richard Sheldon here. Wot can I do yer for?"

'Lucas here. What happened in Morecambe?'

'Total disaster! There were busloads of coppers waiting – some armed. Our lads didn't have a chance! Reckon somebody grassed us up! and when I find out…'

'When you've found out, what you do is up to you in your cellar. But if you don't find out, not only will your contract with me be terminated, I have a little brown file in my bank vault. It's a story of a people smuggling ring countrywide. Names, dates and places – except mine, of course. So look sharp! Get on with it!'

Thankfully, Smithy's fresh wound wasn't as bad as it had seemed, 'All sound and fury, signifying nothing, at least not very much,' averred English Teacher Amelia. Smithy was sent home for bed-rest. Then Forbes and the Super sent for me. 'Watson, we have a rather importunate civilian gentleman from MI5 who would like to speak to you and Smith, There's a Three-line-whip request that he see you at Smith's ASAP?'

My cynicism kicked in. 'I will if you or Inspector Forbes will be there. and if Smithy agrees.'

'We will both be there. I'm not having sneaky-beakies creeping around bothering my lads without my knowledge.'

I saluted smartly and left. On the way across the crew room I saw Johnson with his big paw on Helen' arm. I strolled over. I tutted and shook my head sadly.

'Ooh look, WPC! A knight in shining armour! Don't worry, Watson! Just a bit of a joke!' Helen grimaced.

'Oh dearie, dearie me,' I sighed. "I knew you Coppers in Disgrace were thick, but I hadn't realised you didn't understand our native language, or are you deaf too? I spoke quite clearly. Helen is not to be smirched by your unclean and unhealthy paws.' With that I reached over and twisted his ear – hard! He squealed like a toddler and let go. The coppers all turned and grinned. Forbesy quickly turned away and addressed the Super with an urgent question.

Johnson, red with fury and embarrassment snarled quietly, 'Watson, you'll not get away with this. You're dead meat!'

Ignoring him, I turned to Helen and asked, 'You OK, Chuck?'

'I think so, but I'm beginning to hate this station!'

'we're not all like that. It's just that most coppers on this station are in awe of the Clowns in Disguise. But I'm not! And, how about I bring you round to see Smithy to show you what a polite, intelligent copper looks like?'

'Is it true he got injured again?'

'Yes, he reopened his wound doing a Tarzan-impression aboard a DUKW. So I take back the intelligent.'

'Love to! He's got a girlfriend, yes? The whole station's buzzing.'

'I reckon so, you may not get to meet her, but you will meet a retired teacher who's a lady, a dragon and a big softie all at the same time.'

'That sounds like Mrs Giles. She left me trembling when I was caught smoking, but she was an endless comfort when my Dad died. I'd love to see her again.'

Smithy agreed to see the MI5 officer immediately, 'After all, I've nothing better to do!' he sighed theatrically.

'It's your own daft fault, you great gormless lug! Should have listened to Uncle Bill!'

'But,' Smithy ignored me, 'I want Amelia to sit in with us – after all we'll tell her everything, anyway.' That Smith, no sense of authority. I doubt he'll ever make Sergeant.

After a bit of haggling, backed up by Forbes and the Super, MI5 gave in. 'But she'll have to sign the Official Secrets Act!'

'That lady was a secondary school teacher and unofficial counsellor for thirty years. She knows more secrets than you've has gin-and-tonics, lad!' from the Super.

The MI5 officer, named Compton-Crawford duly appeared in Smithy's bedsit. He was dressed to kill. Knowing MI5, perhaps literally. Hand-made Italian boots, sharp but conservative suit, velvet-collar jacket, Oxford scarf and a bowler hat. And all of twenty-two-or-three years old.

Smithy, old baggy grey flannels, collarless and ancient dress shirt and a beige woolly cardigan held out his hand. 'Excuse me not getting up!' pointing at head bandage. Immediately setting the tone of the interview. You can't really give sneaky beakies any leeway.

But the Miniscule Intelligence Officer from Five said meekly, 'May I sit down?' the Super muttered something about Greeks bearing gifts. 'Now this *is Absolutely* top-secret. You must all sign the Official Secrets act – now!' so we all duly did.

'We have our eye on a member of the Aristocracy – a Lord Lucas – who we have reason to believe is not only involved in criminal activity, but is a threat to National Security as well. He has fingers in enough pies to fill your canteen – trade deals with Russia, China, Southern Rhodesia and Brazil. And we suspect involvement with a Chinese triad. And connections with the top-dog East End gang.'

'What has that to do with us here in this backwater?'

'Superintendent, your two lads here have done some sterling work up here. We are aware of Smith's personal interest in the murder of Ateni, but in working diligently on the murder and the wages snatch, you have been able to uncover a smuggling ring we believe connected to Lucas. You have been, Watson, especially diligent in pressuring the local brothel. And Mrs Giles, you have a better information-claque than we do!' Smiling wryly. 'And we are aware that a prostitute has gone missing. We believe – metaphorically, I hope! – that you know where the body is buried.

'So, we believe that the arrest of the smugglers is the first crack in the wall. We have agreed with your inspector and superintendent for you to be seconded to us for a limited period, reporting only to me - MI5 has more holes than a colander - and to Inspector Forbes. It will be dangerous.' He pointed at Smithy's turban. 'But you will be working on National Security, on criminal investigation, and on breaking up a very nasty little bunch. There is the international aspect of smuggling – and…as I said, we think there's a London gang moving up here. Will you do it?'

'Super, Mr Forbes, what do you feel?' from Smithy.

The Super nodded to Forbesy. 'This will be valuable work, lads. Both international and Metropolitan aspects. Lots of feathers for caps. And…' Turning to Compton-Crawford, 'it will get these two troublesome hooligans out of my hair!' smiling.

I piped up, 'Smithy? OK? Good. Then yes, if we can have Mrs Giles as manager and co-ordinator.' She tried to look modest, but a huge grin broke through.

CHAPTER 13

'Where on earth has that bloody woman got to?' Rupert demanded of Richard.

'Dunno. Mebbe that cop has murdered her. Mebbe she fancied him and has run away with him.'

'No, he's still there. Sticking his big ugly schnozzle in where it's not wanted. He's one of the xxxxs who got our Morecambe racket done. And that other cop, my ship's captain said he was a long streak of nothing with a bandage flying off his head. I'm thinking we send a couple of heavies up to sort those two bluebottles. And have a gentle word with Little Joe.'

'No need. We've got Wilson and his pet judokas up there.'

'No. Wilson is known to Smith, it'll blow his cover.'

'Right. Needn't send the First Team up. How hard can it be to crunch two thicko peasant plods when one of them's injured anyway?'

The chapel in the mother house was full. All the nuns and the girls had come down to Perth mob-handed to see their beloved Maisie become Virginia, and enter into her new life. The organ doodled softly as the congregation chatted. In the vestry Masie turned to Marie Clare and Abby and muttered, "Virginia -me! That's a laugh – but that's who I want to be. This'll be my fourth name – but this one's sticking! And, Virginia – that'll wipe the eyes of my abusers. Nothing's too hard for our God!'

'Virginia is just right for you. You're a new creation! Go for it, girl!' grinned Abby, wipinga surreptitious tear away. Then the organ powered up, and the congregation rose, singing hallelujahs loud enough to bring the ceiling down. 'Time to go, girl!' said Abby.

And five-foot-nothing of Virginia proudly marched in her wedding dress down the aisle, crossed herself and lay flat on her face in front of the altar. The organ silenced; the Bishop and the Mother Superior asked, 'Maisie Billings, do you accept the demands put upon you by our Lord Jesus Christ and the Order you have chosen to join?'

'I do!' loudly and clearly.

'Do you promise to follow our Lord every day of your life?'

'I do!'

'Have you turned away from your former life to follow our Lord and the Order wherever you are sent?'

'I most certainly 'ave!' rang out loud, clearly and distinctly in Cockney. Some gasped, some chuckled, but the Bishop smiled and lifted her up. 'Sister Virginia – welcome!'

After an amazing celebratory tea, the Bishop, the Mother Superior, Marie Clare and Abby took the new Sister Virginia into the vestry and asked her what did she want to do next.

'I want to go back to London and start a work there. There are scads of girls just like me living the life I did, and I want to show them Jesus, like I was shown.'

The Bishop looked doubtful. Mother Superior shook her head. Marie Clare and Abby just smiled. 'That's our toughie!' whispered Marie Clare.

'You're a young convert,' the Bishop said gently, 'You might fall back into your old ways.'

'Not a chance! Do you think I'd swop the love of God and the Sisters to go back to feeling dirty, scared and abused all the time? No way! Virginia I am and Virginia I stay!'

'Go back to Acharacle now. Wait six months and if you feel the same, we'll send you down to our House in Essex. From there you can make raids into London.'

Six months passed. Sister Virginia served and comforted the poor wrecks that washed up at Acharachle, sitting with them when the anger or the heeby-jeebies struck them, and telling them of the God who loved them. But never faltering from her desire to drag the same lying immoral cows like she had been from the disgusting mud of the gutter from which she had been dragged.

Six months passed. The case of the payroll robbery and murder was put on hold by the police but not by Smithy, Amelia and me. Smithy was back in action, constantly challenged by Wilson. He dodged. 'I will sort Wilson out when I'm ready,' he asserted. He honed his skills at a club in Manchester. He ran and lifted weights. And he and I continued to take Alicia and Helen out. And we continued to work at the bigger picture, digging away at the local ne'er-do-wells in the hope of a lead.

So when Bill Boyd did his usual gangster-hiss, I responded.

'You know the Kosy Kafe?'

Did I know the Kosy Kafe! Run by an ex-jailbird with a sense of humour, it was the local scallies' favourite hang-out and the thriving town black market. My ears pricked up. 'Well, Mr Watson, it seems there's some real goon up from London recruiting for a job. Don't know any more than that, but you got them bent cops off my back, so I owe yer.' And pocketing the ten-bob note I dashed him, he slipped silently away.

After informing Forbesy and Compton-Crawford, we were given permission to go and look.

'Full uniform,' Amelia thought, 'and enquiring about that robbery down Cottage Lane. Stiff and official.' So we did.

We slow-marched in the door, gazing around. The hubbub stilled. Then a low threatening growl arose. We stiff-legged up to the counter. 'Put away that cosh, George,' I gently advised the owner. We continued to gaze. We knew all the hoodlums – except one. A broad shouldered ugly guy with a bitter expression.

I spoke up, hands in pockets, 'We're here to ask for witnesses to a robbery down Cottage Lane. Lot of jewellery stolen. Not that you lily-whites would know anything of course!'

The rumble increased in volume. The atmosphere spoke volumes – this is our patch, and no nosy coppers come in here twice. A local lag called Marty bellied up to me and poked me in the chest. 'We don' 'ave the filth in 'ere!'

'I reckon you do – we're here. And poke me again and that finger goes where the sun don't shine – followed by your head.'

Marty swung. Smithy kicked his feet from under him. I smiled quizzically, hands still in pockets.

Uproar ensued. A riot surged forward, getting in each other's way. Some tried to swing chairs, but did more harm to themselves. Smithy reached behind the bar and dragged Big George over the bar, dumping him on his face. 'Bill did say no coshes,' he remarked pleasantly, then straight-armed a thug trying to roundhouse him. Diligent use of truncheons soon made a barricade of bodies that the rest couldn't get over. 'SIT DOWN!' I bellowed. Peace was restored. At the cost of a bleeding nose for Smithy and a thick ear for me.

Smithy spoke gently. 'As you can see, nosy coppers *can* come in here. But we won't press charges – this time! We'd rather you out and about where we can see you. But… if anyone knows anything about the break-in there's a pony in it. The bitter-faced gent had quietly slipped away.

I continued to plod my beat. The usual round of making sure the schoolkids let out of school don't get too silly, saying hello to this one and that, scrounging coffee at various cafes. I am big and wooden-looking. This is an advantage as the ne'er-do-wells think I'm thick. So it was no surprise to notice the bitter-faced guy following me. He made no attempt to hide or follow discreetly. He was dressed in smoothie London gear, sharp single-breasted suit, dark overcoat and snap-brim fedora. Gangster cool, but spoiled by big steel-toecapped industrial boots. Ideal for a crippling kick. And the smart cut of his trousers was marred by a cosh-shaped bulge.

Interesting! I thought, *He is either trying to intimidate me, or he's the follow-up after Maisie.* After seeing the Grammar-School rabble on their way home, I slowly ambled up Wood Lane to the wood where we had talked to Maisie. I gently stepped into the wood, followed by Fred Bloggs, cosh out ready. He cautiously peered behind trees, then got irate. Then nervous. The ferns there grow six feet tall.

I ghosted up behind him, whispered 'Boo!' and kicked his feet away. Moving swiftly behind him, out of the way of those lethal boots, I applied on of Smithy's strangles. He thrashed around, turning red then purple, but just before blue, I eased off enough to let him speak and breathe.

'OK, Chummy. Who are you and who sent you?'

Burst of very inventive language involving my parentage, sexual proclivities and eventual destination. So my gentle shell-likes would not be offended, I tightened the strangle.

He capitulated. 'There's a team after you. East Enders. Out of your league, Filth!'

'Would that be the Sheldons?' I hazarded. 'And I bet you're looking for Maisie Billings? Well, Matey, you will never find her!' gazing around at the dense woodland. 'I want you to lie down on your face. We can do it gentle, or hard. The choice is yours.'

He chose hard. I had to admire his chutzpa. But it still got him a foot on the back of his neck. Swiftly handcuffing him, I searched through his pockets. A bunch of keys, a handkerchief, £250 and a driving license in the name of Jeffrey Braddon.

'So, Mr Braddon,' taking out my truncheon and slipping the thong over my wrist, 'I am going to let you go. I will put your stuff on the big stone behind me. Then go back to the Smoke and tell them – it's they who are out of their league. And show up here again, I will bust you for something, possibly breathing in the wrong way. Now go!'

Whistling softly, I strolled gently past all the posh Wood Lane houses.

That evening I met with Smithy and Amelia. 'The pace is hotting up,' I told them, and recounted my afternoon adventure, 'The Sheldons have brought in a heavy. We had a quiet chat up in the woods. Without saying very much at all, I think I've convinced him that we corrupt coppers have murdered Maisie and buried her in the wood. They know their own tricks best. We can clue Forbesy and Compton-Crawford in tomorrow. But watch out. This lot are dangerous. Amelia, please keep away from us in public. And Smithy look after you battered head. They will be back, mob-handed next time. This is too big to let go because of one plod.'

'Super-plod,' muttered Amelia, 'I remember you in playground scuffles!'

'Naughty boy, Watson!' chaffed Smithy.

'But,' Amelia continued, 'I have here a choice,' opening basket, 'Fruit cake or Madeira?'

'Bit of each!' we chortled in unison.

I didn't catch what Amelia was saying about gannets.

Jeff Braddon returned home crestfallen. 'Sorry, Rupert and Richard, I was jumped! Six great hairy coppers snatched me off the street and beat me up! They got a look at my license and nicked 250 quid!'

'Where are the bruises?'

Jeff wasn't daft. He'd hit himself in the stomach and legs with a pole, so he was able to show a whole sunset of bruises. 'And I reckon they've killed Maisie and buried her in a wood.' The Sheldons, brought up on American cop-shows had no doubt in believing that a local police force would be corrupt and jealous of their scam. For the first time they felt a frisson of doubt. 'Get on to Lucas,' muttered Rupert.

'You sat WHAT??' roared His Lordship, 'You let a woolly-backed bunch of plods take out your finest!' Eton and Brigade of Guards raged out of Lucas' mouth.

'I reckon we're hitting above our weight here,' whimpered Rupert.

'You big, brave East End heroes,' snarled Lucas. 'Send a mob up! Burn the town down if you have to! I have too much money at stake! And remember - a folder in the bank!'

Smithy and I were on the same watch, just sitting at ease for our break when a cadet raced in. 'Smithy! Bill! There's a nun to see you!' Cheer, whistles and claps echoed round the room.

'A Sister Virginia,' added the cadet.

'Virgin for short, but not for long, Eh, Smithy, you randy old goat!' from the back of the room.

'Wash your mouth out, you disgusting animal. It's *nun* of your business!' Smithy grinned.

We walked down the ancient, creaking stairs to meet the nun, wondering what that was all about.

A short person dressed in a tweed suit, blouse and sensible shoes stood before us. Only a blue headdress showed that she was a nun.

'Don't remember me, do you, lads? But I remember you. You saved me in - every way.'

I peered at her. 'Oh, I give up.'

'You knew me as Daphne Doors. Now I'm Sister Virginia. A totally different person.' She did look totally different, gone were the defensive bowed shoulder, the pale greasy skin. Instead she was five feet of proud upright carriage, well-muscled under the tweed, with tanned face and sparkling eyes.

Smithy reached for her elbow, 'Come down to the local caff and tell us all about it! And,' to the cadet, 'Tell Mr Forbes we're interviewing a witness!' On the way, I phoned Amelia, 'Startling news! Get here as fast as your old rattletrap can manage!'

Settled in the café, biting into a huge un-nun-like piece of Victoria sponge, Virginia told us the full story. 'And I'm going down to a house in Essex. I want to get as many of those women as I was out of the game and into the Kingdom. So we've started a work in a farmhouse near Tollesbury on the Essex marshes. I go with two sisters into London once a week, Social Services have our phone, and so do the Samaritans. We're already full. Not everybody accepts us, of course, but they have free choice.'

Amelia gazed admiringly at her, 'Do you never get tempted to go back on the game?'

The impish Cockney surfaced, "Wot? Swop the love and support of you three and Sister Marie Clare and Abby and a whole religious house for dirty old men, shivering street corners, getting slapped around and fear of psychos? Yer jokin' Virginia I am an Virginia I stay! Takin' as many guttersnipes with me!'

Smithy was in the doldrums. Coming off shift, I went round to his flat, to find him looking like a cold rice pudding. 'What's up with you, you miserable-looking so-and-so?' I asked, 'you look like a cowboy who's lost his horse, his girl, and got three arrows in his back!'

'I dunno,' he gloomed, 'Are we getting anywhere? Sensei was one of the best people I knew, I've been driven out of the club I called my family for so long, the bank-manager was a friend, and we're no nearer finding who killed either of them.

'And now we're involved with MI5, and I don't trust that lot. I did my National Service with RAF Intelligence, (Intelligence? Huh!) and I know how sly and two-faced they are.'

He was lucky, I'd done mine crawling through the Malaysian jungle, where if the terrorists didn't get you the snakes, mosquitoes and leeches would. Maybe he was overtired, doing his shift and trying to pursue Sensei's killer. Maybe it was the aftermath of the head wound. But I'd never seen Smithy like this. 'Come on you great daft dollop, get up and make sure we do get 'em!' I snarled. Smithy just shrugged.

Amelia had joined us. She went over to Smithy's bookcase and took out his Bible. She muttered to herself, flicking the pages, then grinned, 'Do you believe this book?' she asked. ''course I do, you know I do,' he grunted.

'Then listen to this!' best teacher-voice at full throttle, '"It is by Thee I have run through a troop, by my God I have jumped over a wall...It is God that girdeth me with strength."'

'You have the advantage over Bill and me – you have this God of yours pushing you on! Us poor sinners have to just struggle on! So get up off your skinny backside and put the few brain cells you have left into gear. We *will* get 'em!'

Wow! Amelia's sympathy really is something else.

Smithy grinned; embarrassed and repentant, 'Yes. Sorry, you both. I did get a bit of a downer, but I'm OK again now. Thanks, Amelia. Guess I'm just tired.'

'After two major bashes on the noggin, you will be tired and you'll be far too tired for a bit of this fruit cake I made, then?'

'I'll have Smithy's bit!' I jumped in.

''get your grubby paws off my came! I'm not so tired I would sit here and watch you guzzle my cake,' Smithy riposted. Oh good, the lad's back.

'So, conflab!' said Amelia, 'What do we know?'

'It's flipping chaotic,' Smithy said. 'What was a comparatively simple matter of a payroll snatch and two unnecessary murders has expanded to encompass a gang of London heavies with a pair of East End Al Capones, a pro-turned-nun, people smuggling and drug smuggling, brothels in Blackpool and even one in this spud-growing backwater. Not to mention Micro Intelligence Number Five!'

'Not to mention also' I grinned, 'a suspect His Lordship doing nasty things. It's a real bag of snakes.'

'Guess that's another call for the Dynamic Trio!' Amelia intoned in Hollywood mode, 'They can leap tall buildings in a single bound – or at least jump over a wall – if it's not too high.

'So, what resources have we got? We've got Ade in Blackpool. We've got Sister Virginia in Essex. (Just hope she doesn't get near those Sheldons) we have Forbesy to report to, we have Wilson sniffing around, we have a thug up from London and we have Little Joe to lean on.'

'And I will deal with that Wilson in my time, when he least expects it. I reckon he was involved in Sensei's murder, and who better to bash me on the bonce on the club premises? He is dead meat!'

My gob opened like a boa constrictors, as my jaw hit the floor. I had never heard my mate Smithy; strong Christian and proponent of Judo - the Gentle Way - even talk like that about even the worst evildoers. Sensei's murder must have cut deep.

CHAPTER 14

The telephone rang. "Yeah? Oh, it's you, yer lordliness. What yer want?"

'have you sent those thugs of yours up North yet? Well don't. I have a much better idea. You have a policeman on your payroll up there, I believe. Get him to plant evidence in both their lockers, then let him be standing near by.'

Richard covered the mouthpiece, but no so he couldn't be heard and shouted, 'Hey, Rupe! It's our favourite Chinless Wonder on the phone, wants us to stitch those two plods up. Plant stuff in their lockers. Reckon we can organise it?'

'If the price is right! Tell him two and a half.'

'Hundred?'

'Thousand.'

'OK Yer Honner. We'll do it for two and a half grand!'

Lucas seethed. But what could he do? He wanted those two black pudding eating plebs out of the way before the next shipment arrived at Morecambe. 'Yes, all right. But no cock-ups! No disappearing whores. Get it right or no money!'

'Right, Your Poshness. I'm tuggin' me forelock to you, Sir!'

His Lordship deeply resented their lack of respect. 'You two really are the very limit. My old established family came over with the Conqueror. The Comte de Lucas.'

'What did he do, O Mighty One? Empty the latrines?'

Oh, the awfulness of having to deal with these creatures. But I need their low-life criminal expertise, he mourned self-pityingly. "Just get it done!" he snarled aloud.

Crawford-Compton arranged to meet me and Smithy in The Eel's Heel, a roughish pub. When we met him, we didn't recognise him. Gone was the striped shirt, the British Warm overcoat and the bowler. He wore a donkey jacket, work jeans and big boots.

'Wow! Don't you look like the Working Classes!' I taunted.

A big grin split his dirty face. 'Pint, lads, bah goom?'

Smithy reverted to his private school drawl, 'Oh, you are a big silly, that's Yorkshire!' then he turned all Lanky, 'Tha's in Lancashire nah, lad!'

Mr C-C grinned, 'Touche! Now let's get serious. My bosses think there may be an attack on you two prime nuisances. It may be physical. So watch dark alleys. I've got Home Office permission to issue firearms. A cough from the Met tells us there's a team of six real heavies looking to come up north. Armed and ready. Or it may be an attempt to stitch you up. The character we think is running the show is smooth and slippery and has bent copper connections.'

We looked at each other. 'Guess who?'

'Your three fat lame-brained defectives – er – sorry detectives. My boss has had a word with your boss and we're putting the latest spy-cameras in each of your lockers. Get out what you need now then don't go near them. That will be easy, because as of now, by Home Office decree and the agreement of Mr Forbes, you have immediate promotion to sergeant, and I just need your agreement. If you agree, you'll be in plain clothes, you will have a brief to work all over the country, and you won't come into the station again w.e.f. now on. Mr Forbes will meet you outside. Agreed?'

'You bet, boss!' we chorused.

CHAPTER 15

Not long after that a break came. Alicia came to us with a sorry tale. She was on duty in the Emergency Department when a young woman came in with a broken arm and two black eyes. She claimed to have tripped over the cat and fallen downstairs.

'But I disbelieved her. Her injuries were not specific enough to have fallen downstairs; no bruising in places you would expect of a hard staircase, but when I looked, there were plenty of bruises, some old, around stomach, upper arms, back and shoulders.

'So I questioned her closely – I reckon I've been too much in the company of you two coppers – and she broke down and confessed that her husband beat her. She couldn't go to the police, it's apparently not a legal offence to beat your own wife – only someone else's,' she spoke bitterly, 'You should have seen her! And anyway, her husband's a copper. Her name's Brenda Johnson. I more or less bullied her into meeting you two, in town, this afternoon at three. She felt that a park bench was the safest place."

'Right. Let's get Amelia in on it, an older woman may be a reassuring presence along with two people of the same sex and profession of her attacker.'

Come three o'clock, Smithy, Amelia and I strolled into the park. We were dressed in civvies and very casually; grey flannel bags, sports jackets and open shirts. Amelia had on a discreet twin set and tweed skirt. And on a park bench by the lake sat Alicia and a woman, innocently feeding the ducks. The woman did not look like a battered wife; tall, auburn hair, discreet makeup. She wore a loose fitting long sleeve blouse, smart tartan trews and even on a hot summer's day a cardigan.

We strolled over. 'Brenda, this is Bill Watson, John Smith and Amelia Giles. We thought it may be reassuring to have another woman here.'

'Yes, I remember Mrs Giles, she taught me PE.'

'And I remember you, Brenda," warmly, "You were a star pupil. Very good runner and swimmer. Whatever happened?'

'I had a good job in a bank when I met Clive Johnson. Smart young PC then. He made detective, and that's when the trouble started. He was out late, questioning narks, he claimed. Some of the narks wore lipstick and a strange assortment of perfumes. And If I questioned him, he hit me. It has got worse this last year or so. He drinks heavily, and the violence has got more often and more violent. Until he deliberately broke my arm and for the first time hit me where it shows. And under the makeup, you will see two black eyes. Alicia has been a tower of strength. But I don't know what to do. The law can't touch him, and if I left, he would trace me. I'll have to go home. Desperately trapped!'

Smithy assumed a far away expression. 'OK, I have a plan. I think we can make the punishment fit the crime. Give me a day or two to set it up. And walk very delicately at home.'

'And any threat of violence, ring me,' gritted Amelia, 'And I'll be round like a shot. We'll get you straight out of there! And come on, we'll go and get a coffee while these two ruffians plot.'

'Now, Bill,' Smithy said as we watched their retreating backs, 'Remember my Ladies' Self Defence Class?'

Of course I did. At the station we called it Smithy's harem. They kept in touch with him, bringing him cakes and chocolate and beer. There were the young hero-worshippers, the bold-eyed young housewives, ready to give a little between-sheets convalescence and the middle-aged plump matrons busily mothering him. We set up a plan.

Two days later WPC Helen came into the station and innocently said, 'Hey, Clive, your missus looks smart today. I've just seen her go into a house down the road in Standish Street. The blue-painted door. Does a friend live there?'

Johnson yawned, looked at his watch and stood up. 'Time to go and see a nark about that milk-float robbery.' He rushed out of the station, almost running, puffing and panting the few hundred yards, and angrily banged in the door.

Brenda opened it, smiling, 'Hello, Dear. I never expected to see you!'

'I bet you didn't!' he gritted. He grabbed her by the hair, dragged her out and spun round. And out of the door boiled Smithy's harem. An explosion of women. Theodora, the widow of the murdered bank manager exploded all her grief and fury into a kick behind the knee. He fell heavily, and as he rose to get up they dragged him round into the back garden, where they proceeded to practice all Smithy had taught them with great vigour. Till finally Christine, a tall athletic blonde gymnast, first dan black belt and Smithy's star pupil executed a perfect tomoe-nage, throwing him over her head to land him winded on the lawn. Whence they all sat on him. Smithy and I sauntered out of the back door. 'Well done, lasses that was a very good practice of all I have taught you. Stay still while I talk to him.' They grinned, proud and happy. 'Now, Detective Sergeant Clive. I have a pact I will make to you. Brenda is leaving. No two ways. Your punch-bag is off. She's too good for the likes of you anyway. Part one – you leave her strictly alone. I mean *strictly*. Don't even smile at her in the street. If you adhere to that we will leave you alone. But…if you go near her again. I will personally let the station know two things. Number one that you regularly beat up your wife. And the most damning, that you were in turn beat up by a bunch of women. Who are quite ready to go to Round Two.' They grinned and said, 'Perfect workout, Smithy. When are you coming back to teach us again?'

'And you, you stinking swine!' gritted Margaret, normally a mother hen, 'Any contact with Brenda here and we *will* be round to see you. And we won't be as gentle next time. Brenda, love, we've got your back.' The Monstrous Regiment all nodded enthusiastically.

Amelia materialised, severe in smart two-piece, the epitome of all strict school-marms. 'Clive Johnson, you are the worst policeman I know. You bully, you falsely accuse, worse, you beat up and spoil the beauty of this lovely creature. I believe you are a *crook!* and I have all my old school staff and pupils who would love this juicy bit of gossip. Now get out of my sight!'

Grumbling, muttering, making what we all knew were empty threats, he crawled away.

'Wow!' I breathed, 'Smithy *has* trained you well. I hope I never have to arrest you. It's gone pub closing-time, but there's time for coffee and cake at Dorchester's. on me!'

Brenda sidled up to Smithy. 'I can't thank you and Alicia enough! I feel ten years younger already. And I'd like to repay you. Not with money – I know you're not mercenaries – but with information. I know where a lot of the bodies are buried. I now have gone and got a flat in Boot Hill, and can you both and Amelia come round to talk to me tomorrow, after I've got settled and put away stuff?'

I thought we should keep Forbesy and Crawford-C. in the loop, he was turning into quite a nice guy despite the Eton-and-Oxford manner and the bowler hat. He chortled and demanded a full report instanter so he could show everyone.

Next day we settled down on packing cases in Brenda's new flat, the three of us and Alicia, who had demanded the right to be there, clutching huge mugs of tea and munching Madeira cake.

After more thanks and showing us round the spacious flat, Brenda got down to business, 'He makes telephone calls to people. There is a Lord Somebody that he is always greasy and crawling to. And there are a couple of very heavy gangsters he phones he calls them Rupert and Richard and seems very matey with them. And he thinks I don't know that he has another bank-account – when he keeps me very short of money!' she finished bitterly. 'And I know and I will testify that he has stitched-up innocent teenagers, yet has let Wilson's thugs go free.' Taking out a pad, she said, 'it's all here. And I *will* swear to it.'

Smithy and I exchanged glances, 'Thank you, Brenda. This will go straight to Mr Forbes and another friend of ours.'

She smiled, 'you mean Mr MI5? There's no secrets in this town!'

Startled, I muttered to Smithy, 'A word outside!' then, 'if this town is so leaky, we better put Little Joe on ice!'

Bidding Brenda and Amelia goodnight, I waited while Smithy's goodnight took a lot longer, then from the nearest phone called C-C, clued him in about Lucas and the East End connection and arranged a safe house for Little Joe. Then we toddled down to the chippie for much-needed fish'n'chips. Carrying them upstairs we knocked.

'We're closed! Come back tomorrow!'

'Sergeant Smith and Sergeant Watson to see you, Joe!'

Grumbling, Joe opened the door. 'Can't you come back tomorrow? Wot've I done anyway?'

'You mean apart from running a brothel? But that's not our main concern. We've left you open to keep tabs on you. But it's your slack mouth we've come to see you about. We know Maisie reported back to the Sheldons. And she's gone missing!' I gave him a knowing, pregnant look, 'but you're still in touch. So you may blab more than you should. Now we want to "disappear" you!'

Joe nearly wet himself; scared rabbit-eyes going all round the room.

'Don't worry, Joe. Maisie's safe and well, and far away from the Sheldons. And we want you to "disappear" into a nice safe house on the Lune Estuary. You'll be well looked after, but incommunicado.'

'But I don't know nothin.' And you can't just swan in here without a warrant!'

'A warrant, Joe? OK, if that's what you want, Smithy will stay here outside your door while I go and wake up a very grumpy Inspector Forbes, who will wake up a very grumpy Mr Hunter, Magistrate, get a warrant and be here with a bunch of coppers eager to ease the boredom of night shift who will very publicly and delightedly turn this drum over so quick you'll be dizzy. Then it might just get you two years in Walton Jail! Which is it?...Oh good. Go and pack for a long holiday. I'll come with you. And take out the Service Colt in the drawer very carefully.'

'How'd you know about that?'

'You can't keep anything secret in this town!'

The Sheldons conferred. 'There's something going on up North. Now Little Joe's disappeared. First Daffy Duck, now Joe. Someone's trying to put us out of business and stop us moving in up there. I've put out feelers and none of the Liverpool or Manchester gangs are interested. A boss I talked to said, "Help yourself, Rich. Too much trouble for a woolly-back little place."'

'Mebbe it's those two plods bumped them off.' (Rupert had read a lot of American crime fiction when he was a Young Offender in youth custody – 'borstal.') 'Maisie was seen going into their woods with them.'

'Could be that those lily-white pea-green incorruptibles are even benter than our snout in the cop-shop.'

'What'd be in it for them?'

'Which two nuisances were in on the Morecambe fiasco? Mebbe ruining our operation they could take over. There's a lot of moola in it. And what happened to the stuff and bodies?'

'So, what next? Our snout tells me their inspector may be in it. They spend a lot of time crawling round him. And he's seen lot of a 'gentleman' in a bowler hat going up there. Reckons it may be MI5, and you know how bent they are!'

'We could send Jeffo back up there, and Wilson's Private Army. Let's turn them loose.'

'And kill the cops?'

'You bet, kill the cops! But let's try the stitch-up first.'

'We've a new consignment coming in. what say we leak a wrong time and date, the snout could do that – 'bout time he earned his keep.'

'Yeah! Let's make it as awkward as possible, say a Sunday night/ Monday morning, about 3a.m.?'

'Good! Let's do it!'

We went round to Amelia's. 'Sorry, boys, no chocolate cake tonight! Too fat and unhealthy!' We both groaned aloud. 'But...I have baked a veal-and-ham pie.' Our hungry eyes lit up.

Three helpings later, we retired to the lounge with coffee.

Amelia spoke. We blearily looked up. 'Smithy?' She began. 'you delighted in watching Johnson get worked over by your tame viragos. How does that square with both your Gentle Way of Judo and your very strong Christian faith?'

'First off, gentle isn't necessarily soppy. If my Sensei was around I'd let him show you some 'gentleness!' And the real, historical Jesus was one tough cookie, as the yanks would say. He often walked about twenty miles a day then put in a full evening's work preaching and healing. And he did something I – or even our tame gorilla here - couldn't do. And that's bodily clear out a whole marketful of rip-off traders on his own. I believe in making the punishment fit the crime. He beat up a woman – he gets beat up by women. And it was the only way to keep him tame and stumm. And really, it was only his pride got hurt. And if I am wrong, I'll apologise to God later.'

had been coming a bit heavy on his dad, coming round to his house, asking all sorts of questions about missing persons. Did he have anything to do with a brothel in town. His dad was highly offended – he's very happily married and of clear moral values.'

"Thanks, Smithy. Now, the matter in hand. One of my old sixth form who's dad runs a bookies came up to me with a worry.'

'you still keep in touch, then?'

'Can't get rid of the ratbags! Seriously, though, he confided in me that a certain detective probably thought betting-shops and knocking-shops are interchangeable!'

'Fancy that! I know places where they are - but purely theoretically, I insist!'

'That's enough of that talk from you, William!' with a gleam of amusement, 'but later a couple of roughnecks pushed their way into his house, demanding to know anything at all about Joe's operation. And demanding protection money.'

'Why didn't he go to the police?'

'He doesn't trust that detective, and he may have moral values but sometimes betting legality gets a bit stretched. So his son came to me, because he does trust you two.'

Thinking a gentle word with Mr Boyd may be in order, I rushed out. Finding him in the Old Comrades playing snooker, I pretended to arrest him.

'Now, Bill, lad,' I asked gently in the car park, what do you know about any heavies looking into the shop above the chippie?'

'Mr Watson, I'm scared. There's something nasty going on in the town – with the cops! If I tell you, it'll get back, and I will get well worked over – mebbe even killed!'

'I promise you it won't get back to the station. And if you tell me I'll give you a gentle thumping and a cover-story about why I wanted you.'

'There's rumours going about that there's the word out to get you and Smithy!' he shuddered. 'And you both been good to me, I don't want to see you two buy it. So I'll tell you something else, Wilson's Private Army have been doing the rounds. And I've been stopped and roughed up by CID three times last week. I'm scared!'

A couple of quid disappeared from my hand into the top of his grubby shirt. 'Thanks, Bill. Now, the story – it's a real one. There's a bunch of lads nicking motor bikes and joy-riding. We are looking out for them. (and another couple of quid in future if you get us a whisper.) But, of course, you knew nothing. Now, a battle scar or two.' I hit him gently in the eye, enough to blacken it, then gently in the stomach, enough to show a bruise. Now go back to your game, and call me whatever you like. A bit of effin' and blindin' will support your tale.'

'Never thought I'd say thanks for bein' roughed up by a copper, but thanks, Mr Watson.' And he disappeared into the club.

I went back for more of Amelia's pie. She looked very concerned when I told her of the threat. 'Now, I know you two, you'll go charging in dressed in your white armour. Don't! Smithy you've already been injured twice, and I hate funerals!'

'Of course not, Mum!' Smithy grinned, 'as if we would!'

Amelia sighed resignedly. 'Well at least take care.'

Next day we rang Forbesy from a call box and clued him in. he likewise advised caution, 'but I know you two. Is there any point in me saying that? We've got a new WPC in; very experienced in sneaky-beaky stuff; come from Liverpool City for a convalescence, injured foot. I'll get her to shadow you two. Meet her in the coffee bar at three today. Ask for Barb.' Chuckling, he rang off.

Three o'clock, we presented ourselves in civvies in the coffee bar. 'Any trouble Mr Collins? No? Good! You know Sergeants Smith and Watson are always at your service!'

'Made sergeant, you two rogues?' he grinned, 'Whatever is the world coming to?'

As we left, a striking if hard-looking you woman got up, paid and followed very discreetly. We wandered to the smaller of the two parks, sat down and waited. Said blonde sidled up and sat down on the next bench. 'Bill and Smithy? The dynamic duo?' she smiled.

'We were told to look for Barb. Is that Barbara?'

'No, it's those comedians down in Liverpool cop shop. My real name's Margaret, but my surname's Dwyer – so Barb Dwyer. But never mind. I'm supposed to nursemaid you feeble-looking creatures. What's that all about?'

There's a bunch of crooked martial artists up here and a real East End heavy has marked our card. Forbesy wanted a bit of discreet back-up. By the by, did you get hurt on duty?'

'No! very embarrassingly I was on a visit to the Mahler Avenue police stables, and a great gormless trainee police horse stamped on my foot. Broke every bone in it. I'm only just returned to light duty and they thought a couple of weeks in the backwoods would be a gentle way in.'

Smithy and I grinned and rolled our eyes, 'of course. Nothing ever happens here!'

'What are you telling me?'

'Only a brothel with East End connections, a murder in the course of a robbery, a dodgy café that thought they could beat up a couple of cops, a visiting heavy, the above mentioned martial artists and a price on our heads. So look after us, Auntie!'

'Not so quiet, then! Goody, try to annoy them, I'm easily bored.'

'OK Superwoman, you have our backs.'

'I also have a walkie-talkie radio, a truncheon, a set of illegal brass knuckles and I'm told, for a mere woman, quite a kick!'

'Great! See you around.'

'If you do, I'm a failure!' giving an exaggerated girlie wave, she left.

'To whom am I speaking?'

'Tis I, your humble servant, yer lordship.'

Lucas could hear the mockery in Richard's voice. 'There is no need to be so clever at the expense of your betters, you ignorant East End yob.' He sighed. If only he could get better help than these two oafs. 'But I need your lowlife skills. I am losing money in trainloads by the interference of two oafish coppers up North.'

'We're ahead of Your Lordship! We've already sent a team up there to take them out. But it costs. You're not the only one losing money. We need another grand.'

'Oh come! Two-fifty should be enough for a simple job.'

'A simple job? If it's that easy, you do it! Have you ever done a bumping off? Or wouldn't you get your lily-whites soiled by such low-caste behaviour? Seven-fifty.'

'Five hundred.'

'A monkey? You jest. Seven-fifty or do it yourself.'

Lucas sighed, 'OK then. But I want it done. I want it silent. And I want proof.'

I strolled innocently on my beat. Behind, somewhere sidled Smithy. And behind him, Barb. I turned onto the alley behind a small group of shops, whistling, but every sense alert. It was dark. It was quiet. The ideal spot for a gentle bit of murder. Two shadows materialised. A shuffle. Two more behind. My pulse raced. Adrenalin flowed. I waited.

'Time for a nosy cop to disappear,' gloated the guy we had met in the coffee-bar, 'you first then we'll finish off the damage to your mate!'

These street toughs can't resist gloating. They never realise that they lose the advantage. Without a word I launched my truncheon straight into the solar plexus of Jeff Whatsisname. He collapsed and spewed up all over the pavement. I concentrated on the other front guy. I knew Smithy and Barb had the back two sorted. Sure enough I heard Barb's radio crackle. The guy in front assumed the street fighter's crouch, took his cap off and waved it about. The razor-blade-in-cap routine. I stepped to the side and as he swung to meet me I slashed my truncheon into his wrist. The cap clattered on the floor as I seized the wrist, twisted the thug's arm up his back and ran him into a wall. He slept.

Behind, I became aware of a couple of grunts and a couple of thuds. Smithy and Barb in action.

We cuffed all four together and whistled up a black maria. At the station C-C met us, sighing. 'Why didn't you let me have a go? I'm way out of practice!'

'So sorry, your MI5-ship!' tugging our forelocks, 'next time we'll invite you along.'

'You better had, you three mickey-taking twerps. But as I think one or more of your Coppers In Disgrace are bent, let's make them charge them. Not only does it give us gloating rights, the message will get back to the Dynamic Duo.'

Clive Johnson sidled into the crew-room. The locks on the lockers were putty. A quick bang on Smithy's door and it opened. He took out £200 and a telegram supposedly sent from a Manchester hoodlum and placed them under his civvy shirt. Then he did the same with mine. Slipping out, he phoned an anonymous tip into the station.

Forbesy, all bristling and efficient, went to the front desk. 'PC Jenkins, PC Simes – go and bring in Smith and Watson!' We were easy to find, we were waiting ready in Somerset's café. We walked in, all humble. Forbesy didn't even look at us. 'Go and find Sergeant Johnson,' he told the PCs.

'Right, upstairs, everyone!' he barked.

'Sergeant, open that locker! And that one! What have we here? Money and compromising telegrams. How do you think we knew where to look, Sergeant?'

'I don't know, Sir? Maybe someone knew and grassed?'

'There is that of course, Sergeant, but even more conclusive evidence!' he produced the photos produced by C-C's state of the art surveillance camera. @And look at how the evidence got there!' Sergeant Johnson, CID, in full view planting the evidence.

Johnson was afraid. Watched over by Bowler Hat, Forbes and those two jumped-up idiots, he could not fiddle or smooth the charges. And he knew the Sheldons would be incandescent. His nice bit of gelt would stop. He was facing prison – not a happy situation for any cop especially one as bent and unpopular as he was. The Sheldons could easily reach him in prison.

The Sheldons were incandescent, especially when C-C made sure they got copies of photos of their sorry and battered troops. And the intelligence that their pet mole up in Bradkirk had been arrested. But they were afraid, too. They were not the only dodgy characters Lucas knew. And, ponce as he was he'd been an officer in the Highland Division. He had access to old soldiers. And some of them were extremely hard cases. So when the Sheldons rang Lucas, there were no jibes, just excuses.

Lucas sighed exasperatedly. 'you useless pieces of pig's offal! Some crack team! My Scottish grandmother could do better! But for a start, I wasted seven hundred and fifty pounds on you incompetents. You'd better earn it next time, or I will have it back – with interest! In your worthless blood!'

We took Barb round to Amelia's and told her what had happened. Amelia was furious. With us, for being so selfish to put ourselves in danger. Then with the thugs who attacked her lambs. Then with disgusting Londoners who dared to cause mayhem in her town. She never ranted; her classroom manner was a piercing stare and a quiet, demoralising hiss. Then she said, 'not that you deserve it, but here's chocolate cake.'

'It's OK, Mrs Giles, no danger, I had their backs. And my brand of thugs in Liverpool are much more trouble than soppy Southerners. But your lads did OK. They'd be welcome outside Yates' Wine Lodge on Saturday night.'

Praise indeed.

'Thanks, Barbara, glad there was a woman to look after these two idiots.'

'She's not Barbara – she's Barb. Surname Dwyer,' we chorused.

'Oh, I get it! Now, more chocolate cake?'

CHAPTER 16

'Good morning, Sir. What can we do for you?' Much more deferential than normal.

'To whom am I speaking?'

'It's Rupert, Your Lordship.'

'Now listen carefully and don't cock this u! You know the consignment we have coming into Morecambe next month? I want your snout to spread the rumour that it's this weekend. Get the filth into a tizzy, then we'll sneak in usual time! Get onto your plant now. There's a century for the snout, nothing for you two 'til you've worked off your failure.'

WPC Helen came into the station, and approached me, 'Bill, I heard something I don't understand. The street's buzzing with rumour about something happening on the coast this weekend. Any ideas? Do I tell Mr Forbes?'

My ears pricked up. 'On the coast, you say! I think I know. Come with me now.' Knocking discreetly we entered. 'Helen, tell Mr Forbes what you heard.'

'Hmm, I wonder,' mused Forbesy, 'are you thinking what I'm thinking, Sergeant?'

'Yessir!'

'OK, rally the troops get Lancaster informed and set up obbo! Helen, not a word to anyone. Good work, lass.'

So the troops assembled, local lads, MI5 and me and Smithy. It rained. It blew. It got colder, the lads got more and more mutteringly miserable and rebellious. Dawn broke. The sea was empty. The lads stood down.

And Forbesy and C-C had the unenviable task of making suitable contrite noises to the strutting turkey-cock of Lancaster's inspector.

We motored home, cold, wet and depressed, to meet with the Super, Forbesy and C-C. 'Look at you drowned rats!' The Super chuckled, 'get a hot shower, some dry clothes, and back here in an hour.' A very good boss, our Super.

Returned, warm and outside several cups of tea and bacon butties, we made our report.

'OK, lads – and lass. I believe this was a set-up; a con. After last time's success they're afraid of a leak. So they will have changed the date. And you know what keeps me awake at nights? I fear we have a mole in the station. And when we catch him…So here is what we'll do. We start the rumour that I was very disgruntled and have closed that investigation down. Go now and have a moan in the crew room. Then, Bill and Smithy, you have just volunteered to watch that beach.'

'I'll go with them, Super,' said C-C.

'Thank you, Mr Crawford-Compton.'

'Don't thank me, I want my bosses to think I'm mad keen and ambitious!'

'Thus, lurk on that beach by night. Just don't get picked up as a wierdo by a patrol cop. When – I say "when," not "if," you follow them to their destination. Then we get a warrant and open them like a can of worms. Got it? Then off you go!'

We booked in a commercial hotel, split the obbo three ways, and settled into a boring routine. The hotel landlord was suspicious, so C-C had to show him his credentials, invoke his patriotism, and threaten the Official Secrets act if he breathed a word. And we settled down one at a time to watching that lonely beach. There were the odd adulterers' cars and the occasional homeless guy, otherwise – just plain boredom.

Then, nodding off on my watch, I noticed a set of riding lights stationary about three miles out. As I came alert, I could hear machinery noises on the breeze. 'Bill to Smithy,'

'Go ahead, Bill.'

'don't get excited, but I think the fish has bitten and the fleet's coming in. so you two get out of your pits and get awake.'

'Roger!'

'He's not here, so get ready.' The only answer was a groan.

I kept my Zeiss Ikon binoculars on the riding lights. It was too dark to see much, but there was movement. Then I made out a splash, and the wind carried engine-noises nearer and nearer.

'Showtime, guys. Something's heading beachward!'

C-C came on. 'Bill, Smithy will pick you up after they pass. I'll follow, then we'll leapfrog. My boss has alerted the Navy, there should be a discreet frigate within the hour.'

'Aha! A fleet of lorries has just pulled up. I'm noting as many number plates as I can. We're in business!'

Smithy came on, 'I'm just phoning the nick, then I'm on my way.'

The DUKW glided ashore. They'd got a much better one than the one we captured, the ramp went down and a bunch of dejected-looking people carrying suitcases and bundles were chivvied down the ramp, across the wet beach and into the lorries. I crouched even lower as the lorries started with bangs and belches of blue smoke.

When the last one had gone, I stiffly arose to my feet and hobbled off to meet Smithy. C-C was ahead in a battered old Morris Minor at a wide distance. We followed, in an equally decrepit Vauxhall Creasta, occasionally pulling in front, then dropping back. We didn't have far to go. The lorries pulled up outside a ramshackle farmhouse on the outskirts of Fleetwood. We parked a few hundred yards away, proceeded on foot, and lurked. As it was now light, C-C got out his Leica 35mm camera and took extensive photographs. We noted down the Ordnance Survey map co-ordinates, and headed back to Morecambe, then got on the phone, double-quick.

The Super was delighted, and straight on the phone to the Lancaster Super even as the local Photo Services printed the shots. 'Admitted! We did muck it up last time, Fred. But we have photos, lorry numbers, and a location. I'll teleprint them to you straight away. But we need to act now, before they disperse.'

C-C whispered, 'as soon as the phone's free, I'll ring Five and get them to confirm this lot. Maybe teleprint them the info as well.

'Well, Your Lordliness!' Rupert was his old cocky self, 'The ducks have landed – a huge amount of the fruit of the poppy, and forty-eight warm bodies. Two died and are experiencing the bottom of the Irish Sea.'

'Well done. Now I'll release some expenses-only cash.'

Rupert snarled, but said nothing. They appreciated His Lordship's work and payments.'

The police don't normally move fast, but this time, with Five booting them up the rear, they were fully booted and spurred and ready to go in twelve hours, C-C and us two mere sergeants leading.

3am, the shouts began, 'POLICE! OPEN UP! NOW!' Chaos ensured; sledgehammers wielded, a surging blue line of hefty coppers charged in, fleeing bodies were grabbed. Police dogs barked and grabbed the arms of anyone in civvies. Cries resounded in at least three languages, and struggling bodies quickly handcuffed.

'Who owns this farm,' bellowed the Lancaster inspector, more of a puffed-up turkey-cock than ever.

A muttering old man in grubby stiped pyjamas, boots and old army greatcoat; looked about a hundred, shuffled sullenly forward, with a grey haired bent old woman, overcoat over flannelette passion-killer nightie, muttering imprecations and shooting venomous glances at us.

'You do not have to say anything…' began the inspector, when C-C stepped forward. 'Sorry, inspector, please question all the others, but these two are Five's bag. I really do apologise, but this is a National Security matter. I will recommend to my bosses and your bosses that your speed, competence and professionalism go onto your record card.' Turkey cock's outrage turned into satisfaction. But the old man staggered and a PC had to catch him falling. The old woman snarled and tried to bite an MI5 man.

CHAPTER 17

'They did WHAT???' screamed Lord Lucas, 'The police have broken the whole set up? Farmhouse?'

'Everything.'

'There must have been a leak. At least it can't be you two,' regretfully, 'but I wonder...about your bent copper.'

'It must be,' Rupert muttered relievedly.

'So deal!'

Two young lads in wellies, giggling, secretly out of the house, nets and jamjars at the ready made their way through the pre-dawn dark to go fishing in the park lake.

They paddled into the water. Then screamed. A body lay wallowing in the early morning ripples. Dropping nets and jars, they ran – straight into a patrolling bobby.

'what's the problem, lads? What have you two been up to?'

'It...it...it's a...a...a...BODY, Sir!'

A bit disbelieving, but noticing how agitated and upset the lads were, he accompanied them. There, lying face down in the water was the body of the most unpopular detective in the station.

'Lads, get off home! I know where you live! Have your parents got telephones? Then get them to ring the station. Give them my police number – it's PC 152! Now go!' He turned the body over and tried resuscitation. But the body was very cold. And he knew who it was.

There was uproar in the station. Johnson may have been a fat corrupt lazy slug, but he was one of ours.

As soon as we could, we went round to Amelia's. she was shocked but not surprised. 'We knew he was bent. We suspected the bad information came from him about the non-landing. And I think he was our leaky tap. I'll go round and support Brenda after the Super has broken the news to her.'

'I think…' said Smithy thoughtfully, 'that there's a pipeline going from this station right back to London…I suspect but no proof that Wilson's army is in on it. We've got those four thugs banged up, but Wilson has others. And what about our other Clowns in Disgrace?'

'Now believe me!' sternly warned Amelia, 'you two are next on their agenda. You've caused them too much trouble and loss of face. They will be out to get you!'

We smiled placatingly. Amelia snarled and said, 'but you won't take any notice will you? Barb's gone back to Liverpool. And the rest of the station aren't that aware of how deep in the clag you are up to.' Then she gave a rueful smile, 'and if you get yourselves murdered, I'll never speak to you again!'

'These two toy soldiers have caused us a lot of grief,' intoned Lord Lucas. They have lost me two consignments. And they just won't shut up about that bank raid and the foreigner's murder. And your pathetic cowboys keep getting chewed up and spat out by a pair of yokel plods. Time you got some real hard men instead of the sissies you've got!'

Both Sheldons fumed. 'you go up there an' sort 'em if you're that good, *Your Lordship!*'

'I provide the brains. I hired you to provide the brawn. And I don't know why I bothered!' and slammed the phone down.

But it was a very different Lord Lucas that answered the next phone call. An almost-unaccented voice demanded, 'Lucas!'

'Yes, Mr Lee?'

'What happened to my last two consignments, Lord Lucas?'

'Er, they were hijacked.'

'They weren't hijacked. They ended up in the hands of the police.'

'I believe the police are very corrupt up there, Sir.'

'I thought you paid them.'

'Only one.'

'just *one?* I pay you all that money to bribe just one – *just one?* Are you sure that *you* are not the hijacker, Lord Lucas?'

Incoherent splutterings followed.

'Get me my money back, or the goods, or you will be paid a visit by my Oriental friends.' Lucas slammed the phone down.

Those oriental friends were feared throughout the whole criminal element of London. Whilst the Sheldons were ruthless in their pursuit of their empire, this tong made them pale into insignificance. And they were the goon hit-squad for the mastermind behind Lucas' criminality. These shadowy figures ultimately ran many of the girls, gambling, drugs and illegal immigrant workers over London and many other places in Britain. The Sheldons weren't afraid of Lucas, considering him a pampered windbag. But they were deadly afraid of the forces behind him. They had tried to get an in to the tongs. The emissary they sent, with bribes and offers came back to them – in pieces.

Richard, teaming with anger, fear and frustration stamped out of the office and snarled at a minion, 'what's the best whore in our stable? Go get her for me! Now!' Rupert went off to seek his own recreation.

Sister Virginia, now dressed in regular nun's habit and a simple headdress was on her weekly evening round in the lanes and alleys of Soho. The habit showed not only what she was, but what she wasn't. many of the girls, especially the easter European refugees had a smattering of religion and would respect a nun's habit. She and the young nuns she brought with her would talk to the girls, giving them food if needed, telling them of the love of God, and even offering a refuge if they wanted out. They never gave money, knowing it would go straight down the tom's throat, into their arms or into the pockets of their pimps. It was an uphill struggle, but very few of the girls were dismissive or offensive.

Virginia trolled down Old Compton Street, praying as she went that the punters, strippers and gangsters may find the delight of knowing the only God and Jesus his son. A bedraggled figure came towards her. She looked bent and elderly, but as she got closer, Virginia realised that the girl was barely twenty and was hobbling because of injury.

'What's happened, Luv?

'don't want to talk about it!'

'OK. You needn't, but you need medical attention.'

'What would you know,' snarling, 'you God-bothering nuns hiding behind your uniform?'

'You're a pro, ain't yer?'

'So what? What do you know?'

'I was a prozzy myself, but three kind people took all my nonsense and my trying to stitch them up, and showed me a better way. This way!' pointing to her habit.

The girl's head lifted. 'I don't believe yer. We're damned!'

'Believe it! You're only damned if you let yourself be damned.'

'Why bother with the likes of me?'

'Because I know where you're coming from. And I was rescued. And God showed me he loved me, and changed me totally. I told you I was a pro. I was a stitcher-up of innocent-ish people. I tried to seduce a couple of coppers. They and their honorary auntie forgave me and sent me off to be clean. It worked! Guess my name now?'

'Dunno.'

'Virginia! That's a laugh innit? But I am a virgin – for the second time! But tell me what happened to you? You're covered in blood, your eyes are black and you're walking like you've been given a kicking.'

'You won't of heard of a couple of psychos called Sheldon.'

Virginia repressed a shudder. 'My bosses till I got out of that life. They are serious harm. I had to change my name and run to get away.'

'I can see by your face you're not lying. Oh! I wish I could. That bastard Richard has had bad news and needed a punchbag. You see it! I ran away but I was half dead when you stopped.'

'Do you want out? Let me take you out of London?'

'Do I ever? I daren't go back, and they have snouts all over.'

'Come with me – we have transport near here. We'll take you to our nunnery near Southend in Essex – if you want.'

'Please do!' I'm scared of you but I need out.'

'Why're you scared?'

'There's something shiny about you. Like an angel.'

'I'm certainly not one. But I am here to help. What's your name?'

'Joanne de France.'

'No, real name?'

'Joan Higson.'

'OK, Joan, we're off.'

They staggered back slowly and painfully back, Joan groaning at every step, to the old ex-army blue-painted three-tonner. The other girls were already back, and twittered and fussed over Joan, helping her over the tailboard and cleaning up her wounds with damp cloths. The journey was bumpy and cold, and Sister Agatha drove like Stirling Moss. Joan felt every bump, but at last they were there.

Mother Prioress welcomed Joan with a tender hug, despatched her off to the refectory for soup and bacon sarnies, then she was patched up and put in a guest cell. 'We'll talk tomorrow,' Mother promised.

CHAPTER 18

Richard returned home much happier, having exorcised his demon on that little whore Joanne. He knew Rupert would comeback satisfied from his all-male club.

It wasn't to last long. A snout was ushered in by a bouncer, 'She's got some news, Boss.'

'Out with it girl!'

'I just seen your Joanne de wottever being carried along by a nun. They got into an old army lorry with a whole bunch of black crows. That worth a fiver?'

Absently, he took a fiver off a fat roll and passed it over. 'thanks, Girl. Go buy yerself some stockings.'

Rupert came in grinning. Richard snarled, 'wipe yer smile, Bro' we got another problem. That tom I bashed has been kidnapped by nuns!'

Rupert let out a yell of laughter, 'Yippee! Nuns with guns! Sisters with Stens! Who was it, Sister Capone?'

'Shut yer stupid face and listen. She was picked up by a black crow and drove off in a lorry! Too many have gone missing. We can't afford to lose another one. There's already other teams want to move in on us. We'll lose respect!'

'OK, Bro – tomorrow the feelers go out – can't be many lorry-driving nuns – unless it's another team in drag. We'll find them!'

Joan woke up aching in places she never thought she had places. She was greeted by Sister Teresa with a cup of tea and porridge. 'Thought porridge might be easier, your jaw looks very hurt. Then Mother would like to see you.'

Breakfast over, Joan crawled out of bed and found clothes her size, cleaned and pressed neatly folded on a chair.

There came a knock. In the doorway stood Mother Angelica and Sister Virginia. 'How are you feeling, you poor love?' asked Mother. Joan did a double-take. She had expected a stern lecture about the wages of sin by a stern black figure – and all she got was a warm enquiry about her health from a sprightly seventy-year-old dressed in tweed skirt and jumper.

Joan muttered something about not too bad, thanks, when really she wanted to scream in pain.

'Of course, we don't believe you,' grinned Virginia, 'you can't get a beating from that animal and not ache like fury. So here's a couple of the morphine tablets we keep for special occasions. Gulp, 'em down, girl, then if you're up to it can we talk?'

'Sure, I'm as ready as I'm going to be. I hate that animal! I've been hit before but never like that. And he enjoyed every rotten minute of it. The for good measure he raped me.'

Mother put her arm round her. 'We have two positive things to do. First, when you're up to it, we want to ask you as much as possible about the Sheldons. Then we have to get you away from here. It's too near London and our lorry is known.

Virginia said encouragingly, 'of course, we don't do anything you don't want – you could walk out of here now! But if you want free of this lot we have a house in the Highlands – it's where I was sent, and it got me round. Sister Marie Clare and sister Abby are the most caring people you could ever meet.'

Oh what the hell' she thought, *why not?* 'Yes please' she articulated through a torn mouth.

'This is what we'll do then, if you agree. Our local village priest – Father Brown – nothing to do with G.K. Chesterton,' Joan just looked dumb – she'd never heard of him. 'He goes up to Ampleforth College on retreat, happily next week. I'm sure he'd take you and drop you off at York Station. The lasses will meet you off the train in Fort William. That OK?'

She nodded sleepily as the morphine cut in.

Joan told Virginia all she knew about the Sheldons. 'While he was crippling me he kept mouthing about a Lord Look…something - and about Chinese triads. Apparently they weren't very happy with them. He was muttering big-time stuff – drugs and people smuggling up North. He gabbled non-stop about his Swiss accounts and some hayseed cops and an old decrepit teacher who were spoiling everything. He burbled about sending hired killers up to sort 'em out. I don't think he expected me to live!' crying uncontrollably, 'and I may not have done if not for Ginny here.' She told all she could, then fell asleep again. Mother and Virginia prayed for her soul and her body, then tiptoed away.

Virginia went down to the local phone box – better not use the priory phone. Sense of humour rising, she asked, 'May I speak to PC Watson please? I'm a nun and I want to speak with him about his black soul!' the whistles and cheers echoed round the station

'Hullo?' I questioned, wondering.

'Hi, Bill, it's me. You knew me as Daphne Doors, but now I'm Sister Virginia. Get out of there to a phone box and bring a pad and a pencil.'

CHAPTER 19

Greatly puzzled, I hoofed it to the phone box down on the railway station and phone the given number. 'What the deuce is going on? Who is Sister Virginia? The only Daphne Doors I know was a tom in the pay of the Sheldon Brothers.' I teased

'Too long a story, Bill, but remember you sent me up to Acharachle? Things happened and now I am Sister Virginia. I will write you. But this is urgent – the Sheldons have taken a contract out on you and Smithy, and I don't think Amelia's that safe either!

'Now listen...' and Virginia rattled off all that Joan had told her, 'and I'm scared for Joan, she may have been seen getting in our lorry with us... and we're well known, and quite close to London. She has had a very brutal beating, so as soon as she's fit to travel, she's away up to Scotland!'

'Great stuff, Sister – even if you did deliberately wind the oafs at the station up! Stay in touch, and be very careful yourself. If I ring the Sister House and say, "Train Station," run out to the phone box and phone me at this number,' rattling off the phone box number, 'and thanks...this is getting heavy.'

'I'll walk as delicately as Agag!'

'Walk what like who?'

'It's in the Bible, you heathen! Smithy would know!'

Now I really knew she really was a nun.

'Sheldons here. We've got a problem. One of our best toms has been kidnapped by nuns.'

'Oh yes??...' Lucas drawled, 'battledress habits? Tin helmets? Webley side-arms??'

Richard ground his teeth. 'Don't try to be funny yer almighty lordship, yer aint got the ability. This is serious. She knows a lot of our goings-on. I was going to kill her but she slipped out when I went for a pee.'

'Well, find her! We can't have feral prostitutes roaming wild.' Lucas chuckled at his own wit.

'The word's out with all her mates on the streets. Twenty five quid for information. But I wanted to keep you clued in. we'll get her!'

Joan climbed into the back of Father Brown's ramshackle Ford Popular and, as Virginia had suggested, hid under a blanket. The innocent old banger puttered out through the convent gates and crawled northward. After a long while, Father said, 'Get out now and come in the front when we stop for coffee – Peterborough coming up.'

It was a typical transport café, lots of truckers eating bacon and egg sarnies, drinking pint-mugs of tea and exchanging loud humorous banter. They cheered when Father Brown and Joan came in, 'Hey, Father, can you save this one's black soul?' 'No, this one!' 'This one's the worst – he drives for BRS!'

Brown grinned. He was not a bit like a fat Essex Chestertonian priest. He was built like an outside closet and cheerfully answered the banter, 'OK, who's first, I can give you a discount for numbers!' Joan wallowed in the open good humour and was relieved that Brown was just like a real person.

'I never expected you to look so...human.' She blushed as she said shyly, 'like I never expected Sister Virginia to be an ex-tom! Oh, I hope I've not spoken out of turn!'

We are human us, black crows, we just have dedicated our humanness to God. Hang on a minute – bacon sandwich and tea do you?' and shot off up to the counter.

Returning, he said, 'let me tell you about me. Then I want to know all about you. And I am unshockable.

'I was a school dropout, and worked my passage to Canada. There I worked as a lumberjack. Forest work is a lonely life and when we hit town on a Friday night – anything and everything goes – booze, prostitutes, gambling and fights. And I dived straight into that life. I was rebelling against my stern hypocritical parents – and I rebelled like mad.

'But there was one guy, little but very, very tough. He'd drive the bus into town, but never drank alcohol. Only milk. But hard-cases only took the mickey once. He'd been a fairground boxer, then professional and never lost a fight. But he got an attack of Jesus and changed. He would walk through the town on Fridays, breaking up fights, picking up drunks, and he was very popular with bartenders for stopping their furniture getting smashed.

'And one night, he picked me up – literally, all sixteen stone of me, slung me in the bus and said, "Alex, God's got a plan for your life that doesn't involve lying in gutters. When you're sober come and talk to me." And that's how God found me and I became a priest. Now, we'll get back in the car and you tell me all about you.'

Joan began hesitantly, 'I was born in 1938. My dad joined the army, became one of Wavell's Long Rang Desert Group but was killed in the raid on Barce airfield in 1942. We didn't find out till Christmas 1943. What a present, eh? And it sent my mum off the rails. Lots of American troops about – so I never went short of chocolates. But I did go short of a mum at home. By 1950 the Yanks had gone home and my mum had disappeared into a bottle. I left home four years ago; went to London to seek my fortune. Got picked up at Euston station by a smooth talker who promised me the world. Told me my face was my fortune. She pointed at her bruised face. 'Some fortune, eh?'

'You may just find a proper fortune in Scotland – oh, I don't mean a nun like Virginia – it's not everyone's call. But the sisters up there train girls to do all sorts, and offer a better life than being a punchbag.'

'Who are they?'

'From what Virginia has told me, they give refuge for women in difficulty, battered wives, abused teenagers, drunks, drug-takers and prostitutes. You won't be judged or criticised; you will be loved, straightened out and worked hard on the convent's small farm. And I mean hard work! Not everyone succeeds in getting away from their life, but you will be given every opportunity. Make the most of it!'

Joan dozed. And dozed. And dozed. The route was one long tarmac ribbon, punctuated by toilet stops, endless bacon butties, meat pies and fish'n'chips.

Alex was an entertaining person to drive with. He had endless humorous stories about parish life, but never anything about the unending stream of grime, squalor and hopelessness of lives that church ministers of every denomination were constantly faced with.

'I reckon God must have a sense of humour,' giggled Joan after one particularly amusing tale of a parishioner stuck in the church toilet.'

'God's sense of humour? Of course he has,' Alex grinned, 'He called me!'

Eventually a windswept, rain-sodden Fort William hove into view. And there in the town centre was a battered old Land Rover. Out jumped two young women who ran across to them. 'Hi, Joan, is it? I'm Sister Abigail, and this is Sister Marie Clare.' Both ladies wore ordinary clothes, sister Abigail had a brightly coloured caftan. Sister Maria Clare, a tall, well-built blonde, wore a sky blue top, grey cardigan and tartan trews.

Like Maisie/Virginia before her Joan's first thought was, 'these can't be nuns!' and her jaw hit the floor.

'Yes, we really are nuns,' said Abigail, interpreting Joan's face, 'but we dress in civvies, means we don't distance ourselves from you – and we like looking good for our God.'

Bemused, Joan let herself be helped into the old Land Rover, and, still thinking that Richard Sheldon's battering might have turned her brain, and that she might wake up in a gutter somewhere. Joan quickly settled down to the care, concern and hard life of the nunnery, and the warmth and understanding of the other girls.

But in London, the Sheldons were getting very agitated. By constantly chivvying and hassling all their gang-members, hangers-on and snouts they tracked the blue battered lorry to the nunnery on the Essex coast.

'So that's where those black crows took Joanie,' growled Richard. 'And I hadn't finished with her. Get six of our soldiers together, tooled up, shooters, knives and pickaxe handles, and we'll go and get her back. A bunch of airy-fairy virgins can't be a threat.'

They mounted a minibus, cracking jokes about have you got your bucket and spades? Candyfloss anybody?

A short hour's drive brought them to the convent. The gang hid out of sight, crouching close to the convent wall. Rupert knocked on the large wooden gate. A hatch opened, 'may I help you?''

'I'd like to see Mother Superior,' politely, 'I represent a charity that works with unfortunate girls in London,' the gang chuckled in the background, 'and we have some money set aside to help. And we know you help them too.'

The door swung open and the gang surged in.

'We're after Joanne, *sister!*' Richard sneered, showing his contempt for the nuns.

Mother Angelica stepped forward, flanked by Virginia and a massively built nun, Sister Teresa, convent chef and go-to person to lift heavy boxes. 'I am Mother Angelica, and I don't at all like your manners, young man!'

'Eough, deoun't laike mai manners? Well, you'll like this even xxxxing less!' the gang produced their weapons.

Behind the gang the other thirteen nuns in the convent crept forward armed with rolling pins, cast iron frying pans, fire-extinguishers and garden hoes.

'You really don't want to blaspheme, it has consequences. And…our phone has a direct line to Southend police station. Put down your pathetic weapons and go quietly we'll say no more.'

'We are going to search this place – like it or not! And any xxx who resists will be shot!'

Mother smiled and nodded. With eldritch screams, thirteen nuns rushed forward. The gang, taken from behind from whom they thought were sheltered harmless women, succumbed quickly. Pans and rolling pins knocked guns and knives out of hands, bashed heads and thwacked behind knees. Turning round quickly, Richard got a faceful of extinguisher foam and a hefty clout in the belly, whilst Rupert received a hamlike fist in the eye from Teresa, and an uppercut that laid him out. Mother smiled serenely and said sadly, 'sometimes, sisters, I don't believe we're as saved as we should be. Now, you pathetic Godless creatures, I hear sirens. You can stop for Mass and medicals or get out now!'

They got.

Sister Virginia liaised with the police and gave them an account of what had happened – as well as four Colts, six knives and two pickaxe handles.

'who did this?' incredulously from the sergeant.

'We did!' said Mother Angelica, 'All of us knew how to defend ourselves in previous lives – and we have an emergency plan – this isn't the first gang we've had to deal with. Sister Teresa was a circus strongwoman.'

'Remind me never to try to arrest you lot!' smiled the sergeant.

Sister Virginia piped up, holding both wrists out, 'I confess! Come and bust us for praying without due care and attention. But now, lads, the kettle's on and there is Sister Teresa's cake!'

Lucas answered the phone, irritated that his quiet evening was interrupted, 'Yes?? Who is this?'

An Eastern sounding voice said smoothly, 'Is this Rord Rucas?'

'No, it's **Lord Lucas**. Who is this?' knowing full well who was calling, but being very much the privileged Englishman.

Mr Lee would rike a word with you.'

Lucas shivered. Lee Ping was the godfather of the notorious Three Hand Triad, and his paymaster and – as much as he wouldn't admit it – his boss.'

Brazening it out, Lucas pontificated, 'If Lee wants to see me he knows where I am!'

'it's **Mr** Lee to you, you rude *gwailo!* Show some respect!'

Lucas seethed, first those ignorant low-life Sheldons, now this Hong Kong colonial. Had no one had any idea of what a peer of the realm was?'

'Ah, Lucas, my good friend,' Lee spoke perfect English, having been sent to Harrow, another thing that rankled Old Etonian Lucas, 'My helpers tell me that two very valuable shipments have gone astray. Would you care to explain how and why?'

Lucas stuttered, 'there are two nosy cops that have managed to seize two cargoes and arrest my crews!'

'*Two* policemen? *Two…just two policemen?* Are you so incompetent or are you having an expensive little joke at my expense? Are my cargoes going into your pocket?'

'Well, what a suggestion!' Lucas twirled his moustache angrily, 'I use a well-known East End gang – and they wouldn't dare cross me! And I know for a fact that my "helpers" are sending their soldiers up North right this minute!'

Unconvinced, Lee gritted, 'give me the phone number and addresses of this gang. We will have words! And if this proves unsatisfactory, my "children" will be round to "interview" you.'

Still seething but relieved to have passed the buck, Lucas put the phone down.

C-C had been in with three amazing gadgets, 'These are MI5's latest toys; made with the new transistors. It's a tracking device. Still very hush-hush, very experimental. But here's three – one each for you, Smith and Mrs Giles. Don't ask me how I managed to wangle them! But wear it at all times, this contract out on you is rather unsettling. And dead bodies lying around are so untidy,' with a wry grin. 'but it will keep track of you, and there's a red button to press in an emergency.'

It was 10.30 pm. I was enjoying a quiet relax after pounding my beat around the quiet town. 'Bill! Phone for you!' came the mellifluous tones of Sergeant Beavis, 'Your best buddy, Bill Boyd would like a word.'

A well-known voice spoke.

'Er, Mr Watson! I'm in a bit of bother! Can you meet me at the back of the parish church – right now, please!' he was a grade A scoundrel, but I rather liked the yobbo, so swilling my tea down, I plodded out. The back of the church; the graveyard, was very dark and spooky. I crept round by the leper's window and whispered, 'Boyd! Where are you?'

Then an almighty bang reverberated round my skull, and as the lights were going out I heard Boyd sniffling, 'I'm sorry, Mr Watson. They threatened to kill me.'

I awoke tied hand and foot in the boot of a car. Thankfully I wasn't gagged, because I immediately vomited. Then I peed myself. My head threatened to bang itself off my shoulders

The car stopped. The boot opened. A blast of cold rainy air hit me.

'Eh, boys, the cop's awake! Welcome back to the land of the living – at least for a little while! Yer didn't know who yer were takin' on when yer messed with East End Boys, did yer?' They dragged me out. I felt very very sick. So I deliberately puked all over the speaker's cavalry twills and best brothel-creeper suede shoes.

'Aagh! Yer disgustin' animal!' and he hit me in the stomach. My bead reverberated, but it was worth it.

Smithy, finally back to Judo was practicing a bit of light *randori* when a hot-and-bothered police cadet panted in, 'Sergeant Smith! The sneaky beaky guy wants you back at the station straight away!' He jumped on his bike and pedalled frantically off. If C-C said straight away, it was serious. He ran.

'Smithy! Bill's been kidnapped! The tracker is moving very quickly, and is right out in the countryside!' C-C leaned out of the powerful Ford Zodiac. 'Get in! We'll go and get him!'

'Too right, we will!' the gruff voice of Forbesy came from the back. The car's six cylinders dug in, the 2.5 litre engine snarled, the tyres squealed and it took off like a cheetah late for dinner. Behind howled a whole minibus load of coppers.

'They've stopped!' said C-C. 'We better get them quick! I think he's about to be murdered!'

I was hustled into the back room of a disused lock-keeper's cottage. I could smell the canal, and guessed that was where I was going. But not quietly, I vowed. I slumped dejectedly on an old packing case and groaned. 'Right, you!' gritted the Unclean Stained Trousered Dude, I'd puked on, 'get up!' I slumped even further, and as he leaned over to grab my lapels, I gave him all my sixteen stone behind a head-butt. I heard his nose crack. But feeling mean I then used both my tied legs to boot him in the proverbials. He collapsed like a popped balloon. Another thug tried to grab me. I tried to kick, but then another three grabbed me and I was lifted bodily up on three shoulders.

'Give 'im what for, then in the canal. But don't kill 'im, I want 'im to drooown slooowly,' gasped the head butted and emasculated one.

I made it as difficult as possible, twisting and turning, jacknifing, and being as unhelpful as possible. But as one thug reached over to throw me in, I wrapped my tied arms round his neck and squeezed. 'You're coming in!' I snarled, and took a deep breath as I hit the water. The thug wriggled in a mad panic but the more he wriggled, the tighter I pulled. The other thugs ran around on the bank, not knowing what to do. But just as my air ran out, I was grabbed by strong arms and lifted bodily out, complete with attached unconscious thug.

I let go and collapsed on the bank, dimly hearing the scuffling sounds of thugs being arrested. I vomited gungy canal water, and sat up. This vomiting is getting to be a habit. Smithy and C-C strolled over. 'Honestly, Watson! You're not fit to be let out on your own!' came the booming voice of Forbesy from behind, 'We'll have to get you a nursemaid!'

'Oh good!' I weakly riposted, 'a good looking WPC would go down a treat!'

'Not in your present disgusting, weed-draped stinking state,' grinned Smithy.

I tottered to my feet and strolled over to where the unconscious one and the headbutted emasculated one were still lying on the ground awaiting the ambulance, 'Not bad for a thick Northern plod, eh? Reckon you Southern softies ain't that hard or clever as you thought.'

Meanwhile, Five had put bugs in Grannie's kitchen and living room – and on her phone.

The Sheldons did not receive the news well. They did sent their tame Perry Mason up to try to defend six separate cases of kidnap, attempted murder and resisting arrest, though.

The Super was so hopping mad that gangsters had dared to operate in his manor I reckoned he'd even charge them with having dandruff. And the injured one would be talking like Mickey Mouse with a cold for some while.

The Sheldons were drowning their sorrows in Scotch and complaining about their losses. 'Who'd of thought a bunch of nuns would take out my team?' bewailed Rupert.

'Yer can't get good thugs any more,' moaned Grandma, 'this never-'ad-it-so-good soft new generation ain't got no moxie! Bunch of fairies.'

'Granma, that is not helping!' snarled Richard. 'Those nuns got behind us. And that one with the forearms like legs…' and he shuddered. 'And if this gets out on the street – we'll be laughed out of town! And now a team banged up in Eee-bah-goom land! What do those coppers drink up there? They can't be ordinary beat filth, they must be from a crack squad!'

Just then, a loud imperious knock thundered on the door. 'Oh, if it's more plods, keep 'em out Granma!'

'Ok! I'm coming! Beat the door down why don't yer!' There was a shriek, a scuffle and Grandma staggered into the room. Followed by a very suave Chinese gentleman dressed in camel coat and Paisley scarf, accompanied by a pair of huge muscular bouncers.

'Wot the 'ell you want – we didn't order no takeaway!' snarled Grandma.

'You misunderstand me, gentlemen and madam,' purred the suave Chinese. 'my name is Ping Lee. You can call me Mr Lee. I control the London chapter of the Three Hand Triad. I believe you work for my minion, Lord Lucas?'

'He likes to think so. But he's just a jumped up toffee-nose.'

'We will forget this gang's politics for now. But he blames you for the loss of two valuable cargoes of mine up in Morecambe.'

'Well, the slimy disloyal xxx!' howled Rupert. It was us wot took the beating! There's them nosy cops that disrupt everything! They were supposed to be murdered but somehow my team got busted!'

'I am not a gullible or a forgiving man,' purred Lee, 'I have lost much money and face. And I intend to regain both. You are responsible. You and that arrogant Lucas. And I want my money back.' And with a nod to his minders he dematerialised.

'What did you make of that?' moaned Rupert, 'His Bleedin' Lordship has dropped us right in it!'

The phone rang. It was Lucas. 'I'm not very happy with you two,' he began, 'your inefficiency has cost me dear. I had a lot of money riding on those two cargoes. And I've also got a Triad breathing down my neck.'

'You think you got problems!' snarled Richard. 'We've had Ping Pong or whatever he's called round here making threats. You dropped us right in it!'

'Let's be frank with each other. I subcontracted the landings to you. You blew it. You let a couple of village plods run rings round you. And now you've lost how many men?'

Richard seethed. Rupert snarled. He snatched the phone of Richard. 'See here,' he hissed waspishly, 'we've lost money as well. As well as personnel! You'd better come up with an idea or the diary goes straight in to the filth.'

'Don't – *do not* talk to me like that, you…you…you…*criminal!*' spluttered Lucas.

'You're no better than us just 'cos you went to…whatever posh school it was. You're just as criminal – and you have more to lose!'

'If we don't get the money for Lee – we'll lose a lot more than a reputation. We'll lose our heads! All of us! Those Chinese can be very cruel!'

Gradually the row wound down. Richard had an idea. 'We need another wages snatch. I'll get Wilson to scope out what big employers there are up there.'

They parted on less angry terms but both parties felt aggrieved. But most of all about me and Smithy.

CHAPTER 20

When Amelia heard what had happened to me she went ballistic. Her teacher voice snapped and snarled around my poor unprotected head. I was a gormless great lunatic for falling for it; I was a prodnose for getting in so deep, I needed my head seeing to – and she didn't mean the bang on it - and she was surprised the whack got through my ferroconcrete head! Then she fled the room so I couldn't see her weeping.

Eventually she came back, red eyed but with a watery smile. I got a huge hug, and, 'at least you lived to tell the tale. Now just to celebrate your undeserved survival, I'm going to throw a dinner party. Let me know when you and Smithy are next off, invite Helen and Alicia, and we'll get C-C in on it. And I thought of Brenda Johnson. She needs to feel cherished.' No consultation. Amelia has spoken!

We were all free Saturday, so 6pm found five of us on Amelia's doorstep, freshly scrubbed up. An equally smart Amelia opened the door accompanied by saliva-producing cooking smells. Having wished us a good evening, taken our coats and sat us down on very comfortable armchairs, she said, 'I wanted a word before Brenda arrived. She is extremely depressed, having found out that her husband's criminal activity went further than beating her – and then losing him, worthless as he was, to murder. So be gentle, keep way, you three cops from anything to do with the station or crime.'

'Yes, Mrs Giles!' Smithy, C-C and I chorused. The doorbell rang. Amelia opened to a very shy and stressed Brenda. She seemed to have aged ten years. The three women gave her a huge hug, us lads smiled and said, 'welcome Brenda, it's good to see you.

113

After a preprandial sherry for us and a lime juice for Smithy, we were ushered into the dining room. Amelia had pushed the boat out. 'For starters I have tried something new. I have put shrimps with little tomatoes and some cucumber on a bed of lettuce, and a sauce made from salad cream and tomato ketchup.'

'Wow, Amelia, that was beautiful!' sighed Alicia, 'You ought to patent it! It could become very popular.'

'Now, people, how do you like your steak?...OK, two medium, one medium rare, two rare, one very rare. Now digest for a minute.' Sizzling noises came from the kitchen, and Amelia appeared bearing warm vegetable dishes and gravy boats of peppercorn sauce. Then brought in the massive steaks. We all tucked in. That Smithy, for all he's built like a racing-snake, he couldn't half put it away. Alicia stared at him open mouthed. 'Am I marrying a boa constrictor?' she mourned.

'We'll have a short break, French-style then I have an immense apple pie with cloves, and homemade custard.'

We nattered inconsequentially. C-C was very aware of Brenda's fragility and treated her like a duchess, without being overpowering or creepy. Helen told us amusing stories about being brought up on a farm, the humorous disasters and the chuckle-producing tales of animals which made us chortle, and Alicia added to the hilarity with stories of irritable surgeons, terrified patients and starchy matrons.

There was wine for the ladies, beer for me and C-C and freshly squeezed orange for Smithy. A very pleasant evening after the dark doings of recent days. After my canal bath, I found the knots coming out of my soul.

When C-C got back to Amelia's, he reported to us, 'As I took Brenda home, she said, "Would you come in a minute?" My ears pricked up, and I almost salivated – she's a delicious looking lady. "Not for that purpose, C-c. You don't intend to marry me, do you? Not after one evening? And I certainly don't intend to marry you. So – no goings-on! But I have information that may be of use to you and the guys."

'I disappointedly came in and sat down while Brenda brewed coffee. She had definitely regained her former good looks, now there was no bullying Johnson, and she had not really had much cause to grieve, more to feel relieved that a permanent dark shadow had gone.

'She delivered the coffee and then passed over a bulging foolscap envelope. "I found these when I was tidying out his office – I was never allowed in there when he was alive." She grinned.

'Give you a hard time, did he?'

'You've no idea! The physical battering was bad enough – and getting worse! But the mental chains were awful as well. I was allowed no friends. I could only see my parents if he came with me. He would come home smelling of cheap scent. Sex was more like rape and I feared getting a loathsome disease from one of his doxies. Do I miss him? I miss the mental and physical bruises. I miss his stink – and I miss the black cloud and constant tension. I have a life, now! But please look at what I've given you!'

'I skimmed through. His jaw dropped and I felt a huge grin split my face in two. "This is gold! At last we have an in to the drug and people smuggling! There are names – a triad, a bunch of vicious East End gangsters – and a link to a brothel in Blackpool! Hallelujah! And bank accounts – big bank accounts, very detailed; he was a hoarder, your old man!"'

'Don't call him that! I'm ashamed that I put up with it for so many years. And ashamed that I didn't realise how corrupt he was!'

'Don't feel ashamed. You didn't know what you were letting yourself in for. And to divorce a cop! No chance! Excuse me but can I use your phone?' he quickly dialled Amelia, 'Bill and Smithy back *chez vous*? Can you hold 'em, Amelia – I have something of importance! Sorry, Amelia, be patient, I'll be there in five minutes.'

A hasty goodbye-and-thanks, and C-C was back among us in four minutes and thirty-five seconds. As C-C burst in the door, Amelia was already pouring the coffee.

'C-C, slow down before you explode and ruin your exquisite tailoring,' smiled Amelia.

He took out a wad of paper from the foolscap envelope, and began passing it round. 'Look! Here's a bunch of notes from the Sheldons! And a bunch of notes from Ping Lee, tongmaster of this parish. Including...' holding it out, 'This one!' this One was a note from Ping Lee agreeing to meet by the lock on the canal where my body was to be found. Then Smithy yodelled, 'look at this! A record of the times that a DUKW had landed on Morecambe Beach, with a few complimentary phrases about me an' thee, Bill, old lad!'

'And look at these accounts!' Warbled Amelia. All from the same bank. And look at the amounts! Slightly better than a CID sergeant's pay - it's in *thousands!*'

'Let me look!' C-C demanded. 'I imagine our tame accountants can do something with these. Tomorrow, I'll ask the inspector to let me photocopy them – one copy to the Met and one to my lot of hooligans! And then ask Forbesy to clue the Super in and lock the originals in a safe – not just the evidence room.'

'And Helen told me something as well on the way home. Regretfully in for coffee only.' I grinned ruefully, 'But she's had her ear bent by Godber. She thinks he's the weakest one of that unholy triumvirate. He's been involved with them in a protection racket and blackmail on the brothel. I guess he didn't know that they had links to the East End. And he's having an attack of ethics, and Helen suspects fear as well, after Johnson's murder. But there's enough here to close Little Joe's little empire down – and to clean our house of two stinking excrescences.'

Smithy stood up and asked Amelia politely, 'May I use your phone?'

''Course you can, Smithy, *mi casa es tu casa.*'

'Hello, Mr Forbes? Smith here. Can you arrange for yourself and the Super to meet us first thing tomorrow – yes, me, Bill and C-C? And Amelia? Certainly, Sir!'

Amelia went and got another foolscap envelope, put the papers inside then covered them with holiday photographs, photos of babies and holiday brochures of long ago. 'They'll be safe here!' with jaw jutting.

'They sure will!' I grinned, 'Me and Smithy are going to requisition your settees for the night. OK, Smithy? And C-C, can you get your sneaky-beakies rolling tonight?'

Grabbing his posh military-style greatcoat, he shot out of the door, yodelling 'Sure can!'

CHAPTER 21

Alicia was trying to persuade Smithy to go with her to her parents and be introduced. Smithy wanted to ask for her hand I marriage, but he was loth to leave Amelia while there was still a threat to her.

'don't be an eejit!' I growled, 'do you think that me and C-C and the whole police station and the massed ranks of MI5 can't manage without you?'

Amelia chimed in, 'Go on, Smithy, get down to Horsham or whatever posh bit they live in and go and schmooze them.'

So off they went, Alicia flashing her shiny new engagement ring around. Mr and Mrs Thomson greeted Smithy warmly. Fred was a tall aristocratic-looking man in his early fifties, mop of black hair with silver wings, dressed very casually in designer jeans and a Jerry-Lee Lewis style top. Ella was a very good-looking fifty-something who looked a good fifteen years younger. She was dressed in tartan trews and a dark-red blouse. Trendiness looked good on them. Smithy had his jeans and tatty old leather jacket. He felt disadvantaged.

Over a very rich dinner; a starter of blue cheese potato-skins, main course of steak, chips, mushrooms, tomatoes with a green salad side dish followed by chocolate pudding and the rare dairy cream for pudding, Smithy declared himself very well treated.

They adjourned to the sitting room over coffee, and Fred began, 'So, John, you're a copper?'

'Call him Smithy, everyone does,' grinned Alicia.

'OK, Smithy, call me Fred. But I want to ask you something. I know you can't do much, being up in clog-and-shawl land, but maybe you could advise.

'You see, I run a string of scrap-metal and car-scrapping yards – which keeps us in jelly-babies, but we're having a little trouble.'

Smithy looked askance, but Ella assured him, 'Doesn't look like it, does he? But I assure you, under that smoothy gear beats the heart of a Steptoe.' Smithy relaxed.

'OK, Fred, can't promise but I may have contacts. What is the problem?'

'It's nothing shady that Fred's done,' nervously cut in Ella.

'OK, Love…no, it's other people's shadiness. A few months ago a very suave Chinese gentleman appeared in office. He chatted inconsequently for a few minutes, then slipped in an offer that was about a third of the sites' value. Of course I refused. Then, still smiling, he said thoughtfully, "Your sites are very open – your nightwatchmen a few old gentlemen with a hut and a brazier. I fear things could be damaged!"

'Naturally I refused but two nights later, my Jag – a new Mark Seven was torched on the drive. And since then, two of my lads have come into work very bruised and limping and wouldn't tell me why. And a few more have given notice for no reason. And the nightwatchmen have been unaccountably missing. It's wearing me down.'

'Have you tried Surrey Police?

'Not a lot of good. Tested the car for fingerprints, talked to the lads who were bruised, but they claim it was a pub fight.'

'Any idea about the Chinese guy? Name?'

Fred thought. 'I don't really know Chinese names. Sounded a bit like a doorbell. Pong? Ring?'

Smithy's ears pricked up and his eyes distended. 'Couldn't be Ping Lee, or Lee Ping by any chance?'

'Yes, that's the guy. Do you know him?'

'He's London based but I have come across his spoor up North. May I use your phone?' Quickly he rang his station, 'Hi, Trevor, it's Smithy. Can you put Mr Forbes on? And get C-C if he's there.' A long muttered conversation followed. Putting the phone down, Smithy returned to the sitting room. 'Fred, can you write everything down? As accurately as you remember? You don't know what you've done for the investigation! And I think I can get Mr Lee off your back!'

Fred started to say what… but Alicia interrupted, 'Don't ask him, dad he's very involved with spy-stuff. If he told you he'd have to kill you!' she grinned.

'if you can get this leech off my aching back, of course you can marry my daughter.'

'Dad! He hasn't *asked* you yet!' Alicia blushed.

'Your dad and I aren't blind or stupid, Daughter Dear,' smiled Ella, 'and Smithy has our blessing.'

A very pleasant weekend passed, then it was back to what Fred described as black-pudding land. 'Don't tighten your Stockbroker Belt, Fred,' riposted Smithy, 'you're soon going to have a common northern copper in the family!'

'Dat's got yer, Dad,' growled Alicia in a scouse accent. 'And don't let Smithy fool you, his dad's a general, decorated in the war and is ex-commando. And don't – DO NOT make any remark about underwear, Father!'

'Now I might just have to kill you, Blue Eyes!' snarled Smithy in best Bronx.

CHAPTER 22

Smithy returned to duty carrying Fred's statement and passed it over to C-C. 'You are one jammy rascal!' said C-C, 'how *do* you do it?'

'I keep in with the right people.' Smithy pointed Heavenward.

C-C said, 'Five has put a guard on all Mr Thomson's yard – incidentally the pathetic old boys supposedly on watch were all found down the pub throwing lots of dough around. And we are beginning the process of getting a warrant to look at Lee Ping's accounts.'

Richard was reading the daily Express when the phone rang. 'Have you got my money, yet?' came an Etonian but nervous accent.

'And a very good morning to you, Yer Lordship!' responded Richard. 'No we bleedin-well haven't. These things take time. We're casing the joint, so – it'll be soon. Control yer soul in patience!'

'it's not my patience you need worry about. It's the patience of a very smooth Oriental Gentleman!'

Richard started. This was worrying. 'Yes, his bully- boys have been round here. They are poison! We don't want anything to do with them.'

'You big, tough gangsters! Good at beating up little girls, but run away when you are threatened! You are in this whether you know it or not! They want money from you, too.'

'OK,' reluctantly, 'We'll gee Wilson's crew up. But I don't like it! I've lost too many men.'

'You'll like it even less and lose more than a couple of low-class gangsters,' Lucas sneered, 'you'll lose bits of yourself you can't do without… fingers…toes…need I go on?' sneered the Peer of the Realm.

'Don't go on!' wailed Richard, 'I'm on it!'

The Sheldons got round to planning.

'Easy pickings up North. And we'll be up there silencing them plods once and for all. The bank-snatch went well, only a nosy little Jap got clobbered – serve him right for the Burma Railway. We're tooled up ready – and Friday is pay day. We watch until the Securicor van brings in the wages – then we pounce!'

'Right, use Wilson again?'

'Who else, the lad did well last time. He's not afraid to put the boot in.'

'Nor the shotgun!'

'He'll know where the money goes up there.' Reaching for the phone.

'Sensei Wilson here!'

'*Good* morning, your Senseiship!' Rupert at his most offensively oleaginous, hard cases need to be reminded who's boss, 'we've got a job for you.'

Wilson's ears pricked up. The Sheldons did pay well.

'We need another wages snatch. Anywhere you know?'

Wilson thought…then spoke. 'Hang on a minute. One of my lads works for Staggs Biscuits in Burwood. Old fashioned place. Run by country bumpkins. Easy. In-and-out. Friday's payday.'

'How soon can you set it up? I'm all ready.'

'Easy as this Friday. But I want a bigger cut. I want to go to Japan to study under the real masters. Then the Olympics.'

'How much,' suspiciously.

'Twenty five percent.'

'Not on your nelly! A *quarter?*'

'Get somebody else then!' knowing there was no one else.

They haggled but finally settled on twenty percent. 'But you'd better be worth it!'

Staggs Biscuits clanked and rattled; ancient machinery turning out biscuits; thousands upon thousands of custard creams, coconut delights, Rich Teas and chocolate bourbons trundled past hypnotically. But the workers were alert. Friday. Payday. Down the Comrades' Club for a quick 'un after work. Then a whole weekend to ourselves.

Half past two. The regular Securicor van trundled down to the loading bay. A large Ford Zephyr screamed in after it, blocking it, and four big boiler-suited and balaclava'ed thugs leapt out shouting 'Get down! Hit the floor! Or you're dead!'

Tom Thorndyke, foreman, one-eyed ex-Chindit ran in from behind and grabbed the shotgun. Thug turned and hit both triggers. Shot banged and ricocheted of the sides of lorries. And hit Tom in the side. He snatched the gun away and grabbed the wages-bag, tugging at the balaclava with the other hand.

By now a crowd from the bakery had gathered and a bunch of screaming harridans and howling roughnecks descended angrily on the robbers. You don't threaten *our* wages! Panicked, two leapt into the Ford and screamed away in reverse. The other two disappeared under a pile of outraged workers.

Until someone noticed Tom sitting loosely on the ground, brown overall turning red, but still smiling and still clutching the wages bag. 'Tie those two up – plenty of rope on the lorries – then would someone care to get me an ambulance – and tell my wife, Rose, that I'm all right.'

Wilson went to ground in the Judo club, then summoned the rest of the army.

'We've got a problem, lads. The snatch failed. Some hero had a go and took the money. But we shot him! And we need to go to ground – fast!'

'Got the ideal place – Marshall's farm. It's out o' the way there! I used to work there. The farm's lived in by the boss's son, Young Jimmy. He's got a wife and a couple of sprogs. Dead easy to threaten!'

'Right! Me an' Mike are the hot ones. We've gotta get there like five minutes ago. Superman hero got my balaclava off. Rest of you – come now! Others with wives go home. Remember! Nothing happened here.'

As always we met after shift at Amelia's. After cluing her in about the weekend and the attempt on Mr Thomson's business, (and of course Amelia was more interested in wedding plans than inconsequential Tongs and firebombs,) Smithy added, 'I've been told in confidence by a member of my church – a magistrate – so keep it under your hats – that an order has been given to close down that café where we practiced a bit of martial arts, and they intend to close Little Joe's upstairs room. But I hope you will agree, I asked him – being as sneaky and beaky as possible - to leave it open just a little bit longer, "Matters of national security, Sir!" He was unwilling but a phone call to the Super got him agreeing.'

'Well done!' I congratulated him, 'but I think we need a discreet word with Small Joseph. Maybe give a hint that we might be on the take.' So after fortifying our starving inner selves with Amelia's Scotch pies, we strolled down to the chip shop, waited until the last customer had left, and wandered up the stairs bordello-wards. We were not in uniform, so Little Joe didn't realise who we were until we flashed our warrant cards.

'Now, Joe,' I began as ponderously and plodlike as I could, 'You know Mr Johnson was a friend of yours. And now he is very dead, you haven't got a friend down the road.'

'Smithy chipped in, 'but you do have enemies. You know who we think killed him? And do you know who really owns this house of ill-repute?'

'I do, bought it wiv me savin's.'

'You silly, twisted boy,' said Smithy in his best Goon Show voice, 'it's owned by your old friends the Sheldons. And they are not happy bunnies at the moment. Things have gone wrong. And guess who they'll blame?'

'But…' I cut in, 'there may be a chance of clearing out – just between us.'

'How much?'

'Oh, it's not money, we have enough *money…*' Smithy let one eyelid droop and nodded significantly.

'No,' I cut in again, 'it's information. We need to make our mark at the station. So, write everything that you know about the Sheldons, and about everything you have heard about smuggling. You have contacts in Blackpool. Gather it all by the weekend. We'll be back midnight Friday.'

As we walked back to write our report to Forbesy and C-C, I asked Smithy, 'Does your Heavenly Boss allow lying? Even by default? You know we can't do much for that poor little mug. Get him off with a fine and maybe probation.'

'I know. I'm not happy with lying even by default. I can only make the excuse to myself that I'm trying to put a giant spider out of commission. And funny little runt as he is, I can't countenance what the Sheldons would do to him. But my Boss won't take that as an excuse – so I will need to repent. I'll have to repent worst of all because I enjoyed the acting. My church doesn't do confessions, so I'll go down to St Anne's, I know the priest there.'

'Seems a waste of time to me!' I grumped.

'It isn't. Everybody does wrong and don't reach his standard, but he's a forgiving God; that's the reason for Jesus' crucifixion – he went to all the pain and suffering to earn our forgiveness. So I like to get forgiven. Come with me and try it some time.'

I shuddered in my Size Twelves.

CHAPTER 23

Little Joe shivered. He had not realised what a patsy he had been, thinking he was clear of those psychopaths, when all the time they had been controlling him. He looked back and realised how Daphne Doors had used her considerable wiles to get him quiet and under their control. 'Hope the bitch is dead,' he thought rancorously, 'Hope she rots in hell.'

He left the flat and went out to Pond's Stationers. He bought a foolscap pad and one of the new biro pens. The house was quiet during the week, so he didn't bother opening. The chippy downstairs was open, so he went and bought himself the threepenny bag of chips, a large cod and some mushy peas and set down to write.

To whom it may concern,
My name is Joseph Burrows, known as Little Joe,
I want to confess to running Houses of Ill-repute, but I never killed
Anybody. I want to impugn (Joe was hastily remembering his English
City and Guilds) the Sheldon Brothers of the East End of London.
They have ran sevral brothels in the East End. I can give you
Names and addresses — if you will keep me save. They will not
Hesertate to kill me and bury me in a building sight.
They have also killed competeters and buried them under tower blocks.
They also have heavy connecshons with a Chinese tongue.
I am in the flat above the chippie. But when you come for me

please arrest me becos I don't want anyone to know im a grass.
But Mr Watson and Mr Smith promised me.
Yours Sinserly,
Joseph Burroughs.

As soon as it got dark, Joe sneaked down Glossop Street to the police station, threw his letter into the nick and ran. The desk sergeant picked it up, and being a very alert sergeant, awakened Forbesy at home. Despite his subvocal grumbles as he staggered around trying to fit recalcitrant socks on unco-operative toes, he tiptoed out of his house, leaving a note for Mary, his sleeping long-suffering wife, and drove to the station to arrange an early morning lifting of Little Joe.

There was an influx of eager young coppers, pleased to break up the long boring night shift. The superintendent turned up, also eager to be in on a bust.

'Listen, lads,' he began, 'we're not arresting Al Capone here, it's Little Joe, a skinny nervous rabbit of a man who was chased out of London. So go easy on him. And after all, he has come to us. Carry on, Mr Forbes.'

'Aye aye, Sir!' (Forbesy had been a matelot in the war.) 'Joe will be no trouble. But he may be inviting trouble, so be ready; look outwards. He's apparently involved with some very heavy characters from the Smoke. Out we go quietly gents.' Of course Smithy and I had cut ourselves in, so we walked out in small groups, not to attract attention. This nosy town could beat the CIA, KGB and MI5 together for intelligence gathering.

Three cops sneaked down the alley by the chip shop and Forbesy indicated that Smithy and I should go and get Joe. We knocked softly on the flat door, getting louder until female squeals and a grumpy male voice called 'Who the xxx is calling at this hour? Go away we're closed!'

'Now, now, Joe,' I wheedled 'don't be impolite to your favourite beat -bobby.'

'Urgh. Mr Watson! Sorry, I thought you were a client!'

'Not now, not ever, Joe. We've come to answer your letter. So let me and Mr Smith in.' short pause while numerous Chubb locks, deadlocks and chains were undone, then a ferrety face peeped shyly round the door. 'Come in, gents, welcome to my humble abode!' his humble abode had bright pink walls, a pink lightshade and swagged velvet curtains. And a sullen looking suicide-blonde in the pink four-poster.

'Sorry, Miss, to break up the party, but Little Joe – don't breathe a word – but Little Joe's an important Intelligence Officer. Mr Crawford-Compton from MI5 knows him well.' Not exactly a lie, Smithy, but pushing the truth a bit. Smithy, catching my raised eyebrow grinned ruefully and muttered, 'I'll repent later. We need a cover story to get back to our London friends. I hope God will forgive me!'

Tom was safely ensconced in the County Hospital, with Rose and a nurse clucking over him. As soon as he was fit, me and Smithy brought some mug shots to show him. And smuggled a chocolate cake and a bottle of brown ale in. He recognised Wilson right away, so an all-cars and-beat-bobbies alert went out.

The Sheldons were getting uneasy. Bit by bit their empire was crumbling. Special Branch from the Yard were sniffing round, their corrupt contacts had gone strangely silent, some of their best operatives were banged up at Risley Remand Centre and people kept disappearing. And the Tong was getting impatient. Now, the jungle drums were telling him that Little Joe had been an MI5 operative all the time. 'The crafty little toad!' snarled Richard, 'we thought he was just a wimp and a pushover and all the time he was infiltrating us! I bet he even craftily worked it to get sent up to Lancashire, to get near Morecambe!'

Rupert smiled unpleasantly. 'He's got to surface sometime…and when I get him…'

But Joe didn't surface. After he had been wrung dry, C-C had a friendly contact in the Irish Garda Siochana, who had found him an Irish passport and a job on a farm in County Cork where the large jovial farmer worked him too hard to worry about Sheldons or ladies of the night.

CHAPTER 24

After the wages-snatch debacle, we were busier than ever. The dojo was gone over with a fine tooth comb, and every empty house looked into. Our snouts were put on alert, and the criminals' haunts put under observation — especially the café. For a week we got nowhere.

Then a cough came in. A milkman who delivered in the Old Hall area got suspicious about one of his deliveries. And as all the local cops used to stop and have a bit of a natter with him, he came to the station. One of his deliveries had gone very strange. A farm where he was always sure of a welcome, a cup of tea and a barm-cake had gone very standoffish. The wife barely opened the door, and couldn't wait to get rid of him. 'It's not like them at all. They're the friendliest lot you can imagine. It's probably nothing, and I don't want to put you to any trouble – but it's a bit worrying.'

close surveillance was instituted and revealed that Wilson had gone to ground in a well-run farm near Lathom. A Zodiac was parked in a barn. The farmer and his wife and kids appeared to be under the shotgun of one of Wilson's Army. A twenty-four-hour watch was kept very discreetly from the farm's hedges and ditches. Detectives had been brought in from Manchester for surveillance; unknown faces who grumbled about the cold and the insects, but loved the overtime wages and perks.

The farmer's wife appeared at the door, a thug right behind her, letting her see the shotgun pointed at the youngest child, who was crying. She was fearful and totally cowed. She came out with a basket and dragged herself to the farm Land Rover, looking back fearfully all the time. The thug with the shotgun mouthed something, and waved the shotgun at the child. The surveillance team, liaising with local cops who knew the area, quickly phoned the station. 'The Land Rover's moving, wife driving, going to get provisions, I reckon. Can you intercept?'

Smithy had one of Smithy's off-centre ideas, 'how about we intercept, ask how many guns, and then if I dress in Mrs Farmer's clothes, get in and disable them?'

Forbesy scoffed. 'You, you great lanky critter? No chance!'

Helen jumped in, 'Sir! I'm a woman! I could do it! And Bill and smithy could jump in when Shotgun opens the door.'

'Too risky,' I shook my head. Forbesy nodded.

'William Watson, don't you *dare* pull that "poor little woman" stuff on me! I – just like you – am a serving police officer. And I volunteer. Mr Forbes – let me do it!'

Forbesy paused. Considered a moment. Then – 'OK, Helen! *If* the farmer's wife agrees.' He immediately sent a patrol to quietly intercept the Land Rover, and bring the Farmer's wife – Mrs Marshal - in

Forbesy welcomed her, sat her down in his office with a cup of tea and a cake, gathered us in and said,

'We have a plan to release your family. It's in the hands of two of the most efficient arresting officers I have. Would you agree?'

Mrs Marshall huffed. 'If you can get those thugs out of my house, you bet!' Mrs Marshall, well-built but currently haggard and worried was one of the old down-to-earth Lancashire toughies. 'They threatened my husband and terrified my kids – and I would cheerfully swing for them!'

'Good girl! How many firearms do they have? And it will be they who swing!'

'Only one – my father-in-law's shotgun. And when anyone comes to the door, usually the milk lorry, a thug always makes me go to the door, with the shotgun at my back. The way they upset the kids, I could *kill* them!' she reiterated. 'They also slapped my husband around and tried to assault me.' She smiled reminiscently. 'But not after their boss had felt my frying pan.'

'Well done missus! Here's the plan. Give a PC the shopping list – he'll go and get the goods, so you're not away long enough to make them suspicious, while you change clothes with Helen here, and then tell us the exact house layout. Draw us a rough plan.' C-C grinned fiendishly and said, 'I'll get in on this as well! You're not leaving me out!' and produced a .22 target pistol from somewhere in his well-cut jacket.

The Superintendent gave written permission to carry firearms – all of us did except Smithy who went out to the car boot and produced a nunchuka.

We drove sedately to where the surveillance team was. Smithy and I ghosted out of the car, crept v-e-r-y slowly along the hedge then crawled on our bellies, one each side of the front door. Helen drove the Landie headlong into the farmyard and tooted the horn. She jumped out and hurried to the front door clutching a basket. She knocked. The door opened. A shotgun peered out.

Then the scene erupted. Smithy smacked the nunchuka on the wrist of shotgun-wielder. Helen slammed the door back, causing a muffled groan. Coppers piled in, waving Lee Enfield .303s. Thugs tried to pour out of every door and window, to be met by strong, hairy, willing coppers. As I rushed in, Wilson rushed out armed with a pickaxe handle, to stand at bay in a circle of armed coppers. Smithy stepped forward, smiling gently, 'stand back, lads, I've wanted to meet Mr Wilson for a while! Just let me arrest him.'

The tumult died down. Everyone, coppers and handcuffed thugs alike stopped and silently watched.

Wilson darted forward and punched Smithy in the gut with the pickaxe handle. Smithy fell heavily, but rolled and brought Wilson down with an ankle sweep. As Smithy jumped on him, Wilson turned and hit Smithy in the face, followed by a head butt that didn't fully connect. Smithy countered a straight-knuckle bunch, grabbed the arm and pulled Wilson off balance. Wilson turned and kicked Smithy. Smithy turned and took it numbingly on the thigh. He staggered. Wilson jumped onto Smithy – all skill gone in a red desire to massacre him. With his good leg firmly planted in Wilson's stomach, Smithy executed the perfect *tomoe-naga*, throwing Wilson six feet over his head. He landed with a heavy thud on the wet earth. Wilson grunted and tried to go into the defensive *jigatai*, but Smithy was too quick. He kicked his arms away. Wilson coughed as he landed squelchingly on his face. Before he could recover Smithy slapped a *kuzuri-kemi-gatame*, - a judo strangle on him. Wilson rolled over, trying to shake Smithy but Smithy kept the strangle on, and as Wilson rolled onto him, wrapped his legs immovably round him. He tightened the strangle. Wilson turned blue.

Smithy said in an ice-cold voice, 'my Christian principles frown at murder, but if you die here, I will live with that. It's no more than you deserve. You cold-bloodedly killed one of the best people I ever met and then polluted his life's work, you and your so-called army.' He tightened his grip further. 'I may well kill you. Then I'll repent later.' Wilson was trying to wriggle and was choking, but Smithy was adamant.

Alarmed at Smithy's words and the set of his mouth, I rushed in. 'Smithy, don't let him make you a murderer!' I broke Smithy's hold, dragged him off, cuffed Wilson and dragged him panting to his feet.

The Army looked gobsmacked – nobody had ever beaten their sensei. The coppers and MI5 contingent gave three cheers. Wilson looked black as thunder.

Then I looked around. 'Mr Forbes, is it time to load the Black Marias?' I asked innocently, drooping one eyelid. Quick on the uptake, Forbesy immediately started to load the paddy-wagons.

I smiled at Wilson. He spat at me. 'Get these cuffs off me and let me see what you are made of, you thick lump of a copper!'

Obediently, I undid the cuffs.

Wilson assumed a judo-crouch. I kicked him on the shin – hard – in my police boots. He fell, howling. As he tried to get up, I stamped on his fingers, kicked him in the stomach and as he fell retching, slapped the cuffs back on.

I smiled again, 'Mr Wilson,' patronisingly, 'you're a judoka. Sergeant Smith is a judoka. But I'm not. I'm a brawler. I don't know the Gentle Way; I rough-house. And not badly, I think you'd have to agree; not bad for a thick lump of a copper, eh? And now,' formally, 'Ernest Wilson, I am arresting you on two charges of murder, one wounding, two – no three – assaults on police officers, a bank-robbery and an attempted robbery. You do not have to say anything, but anything you do say will be taken down in writing and may be used in evidence.' Caution over, I smiled, 'and if I can bust you for picking the daisies – I'll do that as well! Come ahead! There's a nice warm cell awaiting you.'

When the army was also safely charged and locked up, we were invited back to Amelia's for coffee and cake. Amelia tutted over us, Alicia, looking at Smithy's battered face and the rainbow stomach he showed us, ground out, 'John Gallipoli Smith, I will never forgive you if you come back dead!' she tried to smile then burst into tears, flinging her arms round him. C-C just grinned and said, 'These two did very well indeed, remind me not to meet them down a dark alley!'

We all made a fuss of Helen; not only had she been a decoy, she had then rushed in, staffing one of the thugs who got in her way as she went, and ran up to comfort the kids and reassure Mr Marshall. Alicia hugged her and said, 'Helen, you're an absolute marvel!'

Gloom invaded the Sheldon household. Even Grannie was silent. She just sat in her rocking chair and tutted. Without their contacts, it took a long while for them to hear of the arrest of Wilson's Army. Then Lucas rang. He sounded upset; ragged.

'Sheldon! What on *earth* is going on? What have you been saying?'

Richard had had enough worries to bother with His Lordship and his lah-di-dah ways.

'Wodjer mean, what have we been saying? What about? What you on, *Your Lordship?*'

'I've had Special Branch round, poking and prying, making allegations in front of my wife! A solicitor cost me a grand to keep me still at large!'

'Ain't nothin' to do with us. We've got problems of our own.'

'Lowlifes like you don't have problems. I have my reputation to think of, I have standard of living to keep up – and I have large Chinese gentlemen following my every move!'

'Well…your tremendously posh *Lordship,* us lesser mortals will just get on with our everyday plebby ways – we obviously don't understand what you, *poor boy* are going through!'

Lucas gulped, and did one of the hardest things he could do – he apologised.

'OK, but remember – we have the muscle, we have our little black book, and we're losing money as well.' Hiding the fact that most of their muscle was incapacitated or banged up. 'And we've had the Chinese gentlemen visiting, too.'

'I am very nearly at the end of my tether. I put a lot of money into the smuggling – and I've lost so much through two nosy coppers. I wish we could do something about them.' Heavily hinting that the Sheldons could do something.

They rose to the bait. For they too had suffered at the hands of me and Smithy. We had caused great upset in the Sheldon camp, my Met. Friend reported. People were beginning to lose fear of them. Pimps were decamping to other protectors. When Rupert went into the pub clients were beginning to make kissing noises at him.

'I want revenge!' snarled Lucas.

So did the Sheldons, but they were ready to haggle. 'You say you're broke. How broke are you?'

'What expenses would you have? I could get a sharpshooter plus rifle from my old regiment.'

'You provide the sniper and the gun, we'll provide the intelligence, extra muscle and transport. We don't want your snobby Rolls up there.'

Lucas bridled, 'I won't be there! That's why I'm hiring you!'

'Then let's say five grand.'

'how about two?'

'Five!'

'three and a half?'

'Five!'

Reluctantly Lucas agreed.

CHAPTER 25

I met Smithy and Alicia coming out of church. Usually, they looked beaming having had their weekly dose of religion, but today, Smithy looked very down and Alicia looked worried. Being concerned, I whisked them off to Amelia's.

'What's the problem, John?' Amelia in Concerned Teacher mode.

Smithy sighed and looked even more miserable. 'I don't know. We don't seem to get anywhere – other than getting Bill kidnapped and nearly thrown in the canal.'

'don't be so daft!' I riposted, 'I nearly got thrown in the canal because we *were* getting somewhere. And look at the successes! How many of the Wilson gang and the Sheldon mob we've taken out.'

Smithy sighed. Amelia rolled her eyes at Alicia and muttered, 'Men!'

'Now listen, Smithy,' Amelia began, 'I heard a story once of a guy who went to knock a stone wall down. He came along with his sledge hammer and bashed the wall. Nothing happened. He bashed it again and again. Nothing happened. Then after forty or fifty bashes a crack appeared. He continued until the wall crashed down – totally destroyed. You, Bill and C-C are bashing away, the wall is beginning to crumble. You're getting somewhere!'

'But now the Triads are involved. The list goes on!'

I cut in, 'Smithy you great nitwit, the Triads were always involved! We've only uncovered them!'

Smithy slowly brightened. He grinned ruefully. 'Yes, I guess you're right. I've no need to get my knickers in a twist have I? Sorry, everyone.' he smiled at Alicia, 'Sorry, love, I rather spoiled this morning for you.'

'I can live with it, and God doesn't mind – look at the mumping and moaning he got from King David.'

With a swift, mercurial change Smithy said, 'OK, where do we go from here?'

'I've arranged for you as a fellow – and better – judoka to sit in with Forbesy interviewing Wilson tomorrow. He's got a posh lawyer coming up from the Smoke. I've done a bit of asking around colleagues in the Met. He works with the titled morons that get into trouble. He's specially been working with a Lord Lucas that Special Branch have been looking at. You don't know this, 'cos I've never heard it, especially from one of my old mates in the SPG.'

'Now, if you'd ever heard anything from anybody, we'd be able to find link between this chinless wonder and the Sheldon gorillas. I maybe could even question Wilson!'

Amelia and Alicia once more exchanged female glances, 'these boys and their cowboys-and-Indians!'

Next morning a sharp lawyer materialised at the police station and patronisingly intoned, 'You have my client in a cell, a Mr Wilson,' looking down a short fat nose, 'I trust he has been treated according to the law of the land. I trust you *know* the law of the land?'

The Sergeant grinned maliciously, 'Oh, aye, yer worship. The law 'as even got as far as us woolly-backs up 'ere. Cups er tea, tripe and black puddings an' all yer worship! The Waldorf Astoria couldn't do him better.'

'There's no need to take that tone with me, Constable!' the lawyer, a little fat guy dressed in striped trousers, dusty black jacket and a bootlace tie looked again down a nose most unsuited to looking down.

'Ey up, Yer Worship. But us bumpkins ent reight good at talkin' posh like you fine metropolitan liars – sorry, *Lawyers*. I even left me clogs at 'ome.' Then he dropped the wind-up and said, portentiously, looking down from his six-foot well-built height, 'My rank is *sergeant*. And if you expect me to show you respect, then strongly suggest you drop the London superiority right now. Come this way!' and without giving the brief a change to reply, marched off.

Wilson was led into the interview room in handcuffs, followed by the short fat lawyer puffing to catch up. He fussily sat down, unpacked his briefcase and said, 'Why is my client in handcuffs?'

Forbesy replied, 'The prisoner has already caused a rumpus in his cell. It took three constables to restrain him, one of whom is at the moment being treated in the County Hospital for injuries. And the prisoner is a high-grade Judoka. Therefore, my orders are that he stay in handcuffs whilst out of his cell.'

Smithy for all his soft and gentle Christian ways can be a real wind-up artist. 'A high level dan-grade, good enough for three coppers but not good enough for another judoka, eh, Ernest?' Wilson glowered.

The lawyer sat up alert and said irritably, 'I am unbreakfasted, over-travelled and fed up with these bumpkins, what is that meant to mean?'

Forbesy at his most inspectorly said, 'The prisoner, Mr Wilson, attempted to resist arrest, hitting Sergeant Smith in the stomach with a pickaxe handle. Mr Smith, without a weapon, restrained and arrested him. This was all above board, and in front of several witnesses; police, MI5 and civilians. And causing a violent disturbance in his cell has been added to the charge sheet,' presenting a copy.

Mr Lawyer, out of his depth dealing with a violent offence, and totally out of his depth away from the perfumed clientele and the genteel fraud that he usually dealt with, read it, grumphed, and sat back, arms folded.

'Mr Wilson, what is your job or profession?' Forbesy began.

'Resident judoka of the town judo-club.'

Smithy intervened, 'Sorry, Ernest, what does that mean? There is no such rank or profession.' Wilson glowered. 'Are you saying that you *run* the club?'

A nod. 'And isn't it true that the last judoka was murdered?'

The lawyer intervened, 'What has that to do with my client?'

'Perhaps nothing at the moment but the prisoner was arrested whilst conducting a raid similar to the bank raid that the Sensei intervened in. Enquiries are ongoing.'

'Mr Wilson, were you arrested in connected with a raid on a local factory? And did you resist arrest?'

'I challenged that airy-fairy Smith to try to arrest me!'

'Which I did, Ernest!'

The lawyer sighed and seemed to give up all hope with this stupid uncouth client. What was Lord Lucas thinking of?

'Mr Wilson, did you murder Sensei Ateni?'

'No comment!'

The lawyer sighed. If only these lowlife idiots would stop watching Perry Mason.

'Were you part of the gang that murdered the bank manager and robbed the factory wages?'

'No comment.'

'Do you know the Sheldon Brothers?'

'Never heard of them.'

Now Forbesy knew he was on a winner. 'I wonder, then, why the local telephone exchange should have logged phone calls from your number to theirs?'

'Wrong numbers?' Wilson smirked.

'Fourteen of them in one week?'

'No comment.'

Smithy leaned forward, 'Now Mr Wilson – although you are a fellow judoka, I don't respect you enough to call you sensei – it makes me retch to call you Mr - did you stab Sensei Ateni, and hit me over the head? Are you scared of me?'

Wilson exploded. 'you?...You, you lilywhite xxxxing godbothering excuse for a man!'

'Man enough to put you down – and away.' Smithy smiled angelically.

'I wish I'd hit you harder on that mincing head of yours!'

Smithy sat back smiling. Mr Forbes grunted victoriously. The defence solicitor sighed, gathered up his papers, tucked them in his briefcase and stood up. He'd had enough of this rough North Country where mere sergeants are gratuitously rude to him and he had a client so thick he couldn't even keep his mouth shut.

'You can't leave me! You're my brief! Lord Lucas sent you! *Lord Lucas!*' The solicitor sat down and sighed.

Forbesy leaned back contentedly. He wished all accused were as forthcoming. He continued, 'What have you to say about your time in jail? GBH wasn't it?'

'He started it!'

'What about the Judoka unwritten covenant not to use judo outside the dojo?'

'He asked for it!'

'I expect that will be some reassurance for him in his wheelchair.' Smithy showing open contempt, 'and I have already telegrammed the judo authorities in Japan. Their reply is that you are stripped of your dan-grades – which is unheard of - you are no longer a teacher, and you are forbidden to practice judo. And I have closed your club down,' waving a telegram in Wilson's face then passing it on to the solicitor.

'Any comments, Solicitor?'

'Yes, I will not represent this man any longer.' And he swept out.

After Wilson was returned to his cell, Forbesy said, 'For someone with your Christian and pacifistic outlook, you amazed me then!'

'I do hold very strong Christian principles, and wish everyone to have what I have, but much Christian ethos is based on both justice and mercy. And when I see unjust and merciless things going on, I feel I must try to rebalance them.' Then he grinned, 'And I did think that if I got Wilson riled he would open up.'

'And he did – like a gannet at feeding time! Thank you, Smithy.'

CHAPTER 26

Lucas was walking home, pleaded with the night's winnings and in a gentle glow of twelve-year-old Scotch.

'Is that Rord Rucas?'

'This is *Lord Lucas*. To whom am I speaking? Need I ask? How many uncouth foreigners do I know?'

'You keep civil tongue! I can be very good friend; very good indeed. Mr Lee is after his money. He gets most upset when he doesn't get what is owed. But he very kind. Make a very kind bargain with you. You pay Mr Lee a hun' thousan' dollas, he keep you alive.'

'Tell Mr Lee I don't have his money – or mine – two very costly shipments were arrested and the money confiscated.'

'Not my problem! Or Mr Lee's. Your problem. One week or very kind offer to leave head on shoulders rescinded.' The phone slammed down.

Angry, frustrated, fearful, Lucas reverted to his nursery years, 'It isn't fair! It just isn't fair!' he stamped around his office. Wife and servants stayed out of the way. The phone rang.

'Lord Lucas! I am ringing to tell you there is no way that I will represent that uncouth Wilson. Nor will I ever go further north than Watford! After a long tiring train ride, I was insulted by a common police sergeant, and my client – my *client!* Just almost wallpapered that awful police station with his guilt! I will no longer represent you either!' And slammed the phone down.

Putting the phone down, Lucas felt totally alone. His marriage was one of convenience, he married her for her money – then found she wouldn't give him any. And he certainly couldn't share his woes with her. Or any of the high-class floozies he frequented. One last chance to get rid of those two plods and he was off – far away from gangsters Chinese or English, away from cold wife and grasping whores, on to a warm island somewhere.

It had been a pleasant evening, round at Amelia's, Smithy and Alicia, Helen and myself. We had gorged on Amelia's Scotch pies and carrot cake, wine for us and orange juice for Smithy. As we stood in the doorway, there was a sharp crack. Helen screamed and sank to the ground clutching an arm already bubbling blood. 'Close the door, Amelia! Put the light off! Get an ambulance!' I screamed, diving to the ground. Smithy was up and running towards the muzzle flash – but the sniper had gone.

An emergency bell clanged down the road as an ambulance tore up. Helen, still conscious, was cocooned in a red blanket and stretchered away to the County Hospital.

Smithy and Amelia jumped in her old A30 and drove as fast as it could to the hospital. I stayed back and phoned Forbesy. Alicia and I washed away the blood stain and locked Amelia's house. Then we too left for the hospital. In the waiting room were Smithy and Amelia, Forbesy and the Super - and a very grave senior consultant. 'She's in surgery. It does not look good. The spine is shattered. There is a large entry wound near her hip. She may never walk again.'

The guilt hit me. If I hadn't courted Helen, she would still be walking and healthy. I don't cry easily, but I left the room and sobbed. Then the guilt turned to anger. I would hunt those murdering bastards down if it took forever. An innocent lass, WPC in a fairly quiet town, much respected in the station and the town, gunned down on a friend's doorstep.

We waited. And waited. And waited. Smithy and Alicia spent a long time in the chapel praying. Amelia and I just sat, dumb.

After many hours the same consultant came in. 'The surgery went well. The surgeon did a terrific job of repairing the vertebrae. A new procedure involving stainless steel inserts. She will be in hospital two weeks, then I have arranged to send her to Stoke Mandeville. She may need a wheelchair for a while, but she should walk again. But she will never be fit enough to pursue a police career.'

I was saddened that a bright capable young WPC had lost her calling with one bullet. But I was coldly and internally seeing red. I would get that sniper, no matter what.

CHAPTER 27

The next day, Forbesy gave us both compassionate leave. We met at Amelia's for a council of war. We began to draw threads together. Amelia made us a chart on an easel. The murder of Sensei and the attack on Smithy. The sudden appearance of Little Joe and the setting up of the town brothel. The news that percolated via the school about the prostitution. The attempt to seduce me by Daphne Doors, now re-virgined as Sister Virginia. The London would-be hard lads. My near drowning. Wilson's Private Army. Now the shooting.

'I really do believe that you two are the targets,' Amelia said thoughtfully, 'it's you two who have ruffled feathers and been targeted before. It was serious before, but it's become lethal.' As we looked at Amelia's chart, it became very obvious that we had serendipitously put a lot of spanners in a lot of works.

Amelia continued, 'Bill, can you gee up your old SPG thugs in the Met to put pressure on those gangsters?'

'Sure - and we need more Met CID involvement, and to bring C-C back up here,'

Smithy thought aloud. 'Well keep up pressure, pressure and more pressure, and we'll ask C-C to do what he can about the Triad. Starting with its Hong Cong base.'

Lee Ping was feeling pressure. He was master of all he surveyed in London, the big wheel. But at home in Hong Kong, he was a provincial little wheel; a mere cog. And Hong Kong were getting restless about their investment. He could feel the cold draught of suspicion wafting westwards, and he felt his head rock on his shoulders.

The Sheldons' phone rang. The bug was perfectly clear. 'You have only three days left for you to pay my money,' came a very suave voice down the phone, 'Then – say goodbye to your head!' The voice was as imperturbable as always, but the voice's owner felt far from calm. Butterflies with clogs on were dancing round his stomach, his head was playing a bass drum and he was running to the toilet every few minutes. He knew what his masters were capable of.

Lucas too was panicking. His world had crashed around him. The Sheldons had had a report from their sniper. He had missed the bluebottles but hit and badly injured a WPC. The papers were full of it, it was on radio and TV news, and the sniper was lying low, unwilling to go anywhere. *That was Jock!* He thought, *Tough, go-anywhere do-anything regimental hard-man. And he failed!* His brain whirled. All thoughts of revenge had gone – now he just wanted safely out. He paced up and down. He wrung his hands, he thought. He pondered. But above all he worried.

Finally a plan came to him. He reached for the phone. 'Sheldons? I've put your five grand in your account. Now, for another ten, I want some bodyguards.'

'What doing?'

'I plan to sneak off to Scotland – a little one-horse place called Aviemore. It's full of low-class Scottish peasants and hooray-Henry skiers. I have a share in a little shooting lodge there where I can lie low. But I need muscle – armed muscle – just in case.'

'Who's after yer lordship, then?' Richard enquired.

'There is a Chinese tong after me, for money that *you two* failed to deliver. It's your fault, but do me this one last favour and ten thousand pounds is yours.' he felt he could be very generous, because when pay-up time came he would be long gone.

Richard went silent. Then muttered to Rupert. They knew they would agree, the tong was after them also. And Special Branch. A few days with kilted hairy haggis eaters seemed ideal. 'OK yer scared lordship, as a special favour we'll do it for ten. And two grand expenses.'

'Expenses? What expenses?'

'You want us tooled up, guns and ammo don't come cheap. You're getting a bargain for two grand.' He went silent again. More mutterings. 'And as another favour, we'll do it ourselves.' He didn't tell Lucas that they had no manpower left.

'OK, twelve it is. I need to raise it, I'm so broke. You may have to wait.'

'We'll trust yer, thousands wouldn't. In the meantime there were those two nosy coppers to get rid of.' Listening to the bug, I guess Smithy and I were having an effect.

Sister Virginia was on patrol in the East End. Her ears were open to what was going on in the underworld. There would seem to be a fizzing in the area like a shaken bottle of coke. Her former mentors and abusers, the Sheldons, seemed to be having a rough time of it. There was still talk of the disappearance of a certain young whore called Daphne Doors, and gossip was rife about which new council house foundations were graced by her presence. There was gossip about another girl disappearing without trace. And wasn't it strange, Sister, that a lot of the Sheldons' heavy mob were being banged up somewhere up North? And a lot more Chinese than usual had been seen in the area.

But then, whilst chatting to Denise, a girl known as a Sheldon Special, (as Virginia had been,) over a late night coffee, she learned that the brothers had sent a hit-man up north to exterminate a couple of nosy coppers. It was an ex squaddie, a guy called Mitchell who had been a sniper with the army. The rumour was that he was a professional; hired by anyone with the money, to kill anyone. 'He'd kill the whole bleedin' royal family if you paid him enough!'

Virginia's heart stopped. 'It must be Bill and Smithy!' she gasped.

'What?'

She pulled herself together, 'Nothing, just thinking aloud.' Quickly she departed as soon as she could and ran to find a working phone box – as rare as an honest politician in that area, and finding one, gabbled an incoherent message to Bradkirk police station.

'Hang on, luv,' said the desk sergeant, 'start again.'

This is Sister Virginia, and I need to speak urgently to Sergeant Watson or Sergeant Smith! *Very* urgently!'

Thankfully, we were both on duty and skiving on a tea break. 'Bill! Smithy! It's yer favourite nun on the phone! 'Urry up, she's in a call box.' Catcalls and mickey taking comments all round.

'Virginia? That you?'

'Bill – you and Smithy, watch out! There's a hit-man on your tail.'

'Yes! He's already tried. A nice young WPC was shot in the spine coming out of Amelia's with us.'

'Oh, Dear Lord heal that poor girl! Keep these two safe! You know what they mean to me!

'Anyway, his name is Harry Mitchell, ex-army sniper. Decorated in Korea but gone rogue. He's reckoned to be good! And,' calming down a little, 'me and the girls at the priory will pray for you!'

'Thanks, we'll let our inspector and super know. They'll put out an order to all cars and foot patrols – watch, but don't approach.'

Harry Mitchell lay on his bed in the Eel's Head pub, booked in as William Watson. He smirked, booking in as the quarry. But he was annoyed. The first time he'd missed for years, as many a gook and a mobster would attest – if they could have. The contract was still unfulfilled. Why did that dopy bird have to get in the way? He'd had to report his failure to Major Lucas, and had got the rough edge of His Lordship's tongue. Which offended ex-sergeant-major Mitchell no end. He'd been up to the neck in muck and bullets while His greasy Lordship had been swanning round HQ officers' mess.

But he couldn't tell him where to stick his contract – word would get about that Mitchell's useless and trade would disappear. 'Sometimes I feel like the guy who rode the tiger – he daren't get off,' he grumbled to himself.

The word went out. All pubs and hostelries in and around the town were to be questioned for any stranger staying there. No easy task. There were always visitors and travelling salesmen round the town, and we didn't have any description at all of the sniper.

Finally, after wearing out a lot of plod's footwear, we got a possible from the Eel's Head, a fairly seedy town centre pub. The bobby had talked to a smart-looking dolly-bird barmaid, (Of course!) she had talked about a guy who had been very irritable and rude when he booked in and had not come out of his room except to use the pub phone since. 'He demands beer and fish-n-chips all the time. And I don't like the way he looks at me.

CHAPTER 28

The Super called a council-of-war. He was all for sending an armed team in straight away.

Smithy disagreed. 'Sir, if I may suggest, that pub's windows look out on Church Street. This guy is fly; a professional. If he sees a bunch of blue pointed heads surge into the pub – he'll be gone!'

'So, Smith, any ideas?'

'how about, Sir, Bill and I sign in separately as a couple of travellers, "accidentally" meet up in the bar and see how the land lies? And if he makes a move, we phone you, and if he doesn't – we break into his room at three ack emma?'

Forbesy piped up, 'You couldn't wish a better pair than these two ruffians for this work. We'll send the PC round in civvies to ensure there are two rooms available – and I think from the way he looked he'd welcome a chance to go and see the barmaid again!'

The Super smiled, then nodded, 'Quick as you like, Mr Forbes, find out the suspect's room and I'll get a search warrant for that room!' Once our Superintendent got convinced of anything, he was a ball for fire. Within the hour, the PC had booked two rooms, chatted up the barmaid and come back with a date for himself and room numbers for us, and the Super came through the door with a search warrant for Eel's Head Room Six.

Smithy and I raided the lost property box and the seized goody box. Smithy drew a posh camel hair coat, a white shirt and a cravat, tailored trousers and a pair of wingtip shoes = a very successful traveller. I thought that wouldn't work for my rugged beauty so I chose a clean-but-shabby suit, blue shirt with slightly worn collar and a regimental-looking tie; a traveller down on his luck. We drew two well-used briefcases from Culprits In Disgrace – our old friends Godber and McLaren, who were not happy.

I went in the pub first and booked into my room, then went into the bat and ordered a pint of Guinness. Half an hour a vision of successful loveliness breezed through the door, booked in and came into the bar. He ordered himself a pint of orange juice, 'an ulcer, you know!' and let his lonely eye fall on me. 'Hi, you on the road too?' holding out a hand, 'John Snell, traveller in Ladies' Underwear.'

'Hope it's comfortable! Bill Nelson, I sell stationary sundries, and'll have to sell my soul if things don't improve!'

We had a polite chat, went down the road for fish-n-chips, and asked our PC's favourite barmaid if Mr William Nelson was in his room.

'Right pair of fly dudes, you two, aren't yer? Travelling in ladies underwear,' she giggled. 'So what's going on? You two are never reps!'

'We'll let Constable Grimes tell you when it's all over,' Smithy promised, 'But in the meantime, keep stumm, please!'

She blushed prettily, Constable Grimes was obviously already well in here. Lucky lad.

We went to our respective rooms and unpacked our respective attache cases; short CID truncheons, handcuffs, oil for the Mitchell's room's lock and a not-altogether-legal picklock.

My muffled alarm buzzed me awake at 3.30 am. i dressing quickly and arming myself crept down to Smithy's room. He was awake and similarly armed. We crept like a pair of ghosts in carpet-slippers down to *chez* Mitchell and after dripping a little oil into the lock, operated the picklock. The door didn't open. The washstand was jammed behind it.

Assuming a plummy hotel-manager accent, Smithy called softly, 'Sir! Sir! Quickly! Fire!'

A grumbling Mitchell arose cursing and swearing to move the washstand. I charged with my not-inconsiderable weight against the door, feeling a crunch as it slammed Mitchell against the wall. Smithy rushed in and with chop on the carotid artery rendered him dazed and powerless. We had the handcuffs on him in no time, confirmed he matched Mitchell's identity, stuffed a sock in his mouth to stop him waking the whole house with his salty comments, and proceeded to search the room. In his duffel bag, under the grubby underwear there were two passports, one in the name of Mitchell and one in my name. Cheeky so-and-so! There was also a driving licence made out to Mitchell. Clean with no endorsements. Crafty and professional, our Mr Mitchell.

Then standing upright in the wardrobe and loaded, ready for instant use was an army-issue Lee Enfield 0.303. not the ideal sniper weapon which probably explained why he hit Helen and not one of us. Maybe that was all he could get at short notice.

The black maria arrived in no time, and Mr Mitchell was safely ensconced in a cell and fed the requisite bacon and eggs and tea whilst the Super got a dozy yawning duty officer in MOD records to look up 'Mitchell.'

There were quite a few, but the one that fitted our lad was a sergeant major Harry Mitchell, trained sniper, served – guess what! – with Lord Lucas. He denied his name and asked to phone a lawyer. We took his fingerprints then he was put back in the cell to wait whilst another flash lawyer came up from the Smoke.

This one was tall, grey-haired and svelte; the opposite of Wilson's brief. But just as arrogant.

Mitchell was brought up from his cell, and plonked himself on his chair like he owned it. The lawyer sashayed in and perched finicky on his chair, staring at us in a manner intended to overwhelm. It didn't work. Forbesy had entrusted Smithy and me to do the questioning, with himself and a newly-arrived C-C ready to intervene if necessary.

Ignoring the brief, Smithy waded in, 'You are Harold Mitchell, former soldier?'

'Sergeant Major.'

'Oh, yes, I did National Service in the RAF; don't really follow army ranks.'

Mitchell glowered.

'And you were discharged honourably three years ago, decorated for bravery?'

'Yes.'

'So how come you were found under a false name with a loaded rifle?'

'No comment!'

'Oh dear, Mr Mitchell, Dragnet has a lot to answer for!'

At this point, I waded in, 'How come an honourable and decorated soldier is in a police station charged with wounding a WPC, using a false identity and possession of an illegal firearm? What changed you?'

'Irrelevant and unproven!' pontificated the solicitor, 'Do not answer that question, Mr Mitchell!'

'Point taken, Mr Errr...'

He looked down his nose, '*Sir* Reginald Stuyvesant.'

Ignoring him, I continued, 'Do you deny, Mr Mitchell, that on Friday the fifteenth of this month you discharged a firearm at Number 27 Parker Road? And was it intended to kill either myself or Sergeant Smith?'

He said nothing but the glare in his eyes told us he wished he had had a Sten.

'What grounds for detaining my client, do you have? And why are two mere sergeants conducting this *interrogation?*'

'it is the duty of every police officer to conduct investigation, as you well know Sir Richard,'

'Reginald!'

'And as the arresting officers, Sergeant Smith and I were given this duty by our superiors.'

At this point, the big gun, in the shape of C-C entered. 'Good afternoon, Mr Stuyvesant, I my name is Crawford-Compton, and I am overseeing this *investigation* on behalf of MI5. We believe Mr Mitchell has connections with an international web of drug-and-people smugglers, and was hired by a well known gang in the East End of London to assassinate Smith and Watson,' looking down his Harrovian nose at Sir R.

'Quite in order with the legal code to appraise you of your client's circumstances, as defence solicitor, I will inform you that further and even more serious charges await your client as certain investigations under the Official Secrets Act are being pursued. Please carry on, Sergeants.'

Sir R. hastily scribbled in his notebook.

'So, Mitchell' dropping the Mr, 'what brought you up to Bradkirk?'

'Holiday.'

'Going to Southport? I didn't see any buckets and spades in your room.'

'But we did find a loaded rifle and a false passport – made out in the name of Sergeant Watson in your room.' Smithy cut in, 'was that an attempt to perhaps incriminate him? Or just a quirky sense of humour?'

'That is irrelevant, *Sergeant!*' from Sir R.

'So do you consider finding your client travelling under false pretences and with an illegally held weapon *irrelevant?*' Smithy, himself from a posh background knew how to handle pretentious burks like Sir R.'

'You are not here to interrogate me, *Sergeant.*'

'In which case, for the record, would you like to proffer exactly what you do consider irrelevant, in order to clarify your client's position?'

'I have no intention of revealing my thoughts on this issue to the prosecution.'

'Come, come, Mr Stuyvesant; as a top-flight lawyer you know the difference between a standard police interview and a prosecution? Because if you do not, I certainly do, and you are only harming your client by this feeble – and failed - attempt to confuse the issue. We don't have time to waste. If you have any legal grounds to refute these charges, please offer them. Otherwise, please do not attempt to muddy the waters with your own irrelevances.'

Like so many posh private school products, especially from the Home Counties, Sir R had assumed that a Northern police procedure would be neolithic and stupid.

Neither of us were.

C-C began, 'it would go well with you if you were to help both the police and the security services. What do you think, Mr Mitchell?'

'Can you cut me a deal?'

'We are not American, Mr Mitchell, so we do not do deals. But I believe that the superior officers in this station would advise any prosecution to go light on you.'

'OK, here it is.' The defence lawyer cringed. 'I was hired to frighten Sergeant Smith and Sergeant Watson. They were causing disruption to my clients of considerable monetary value.'

Sir R seethed. I smiled.

'Who were your clients?' I growled, 'And I don't believe that you – a high-class and efficient assassin - came all the way up here to just put the frighteners on. Attempted murder is the charge! Or are you just incompetent?'

Pride surged. 'When I want people dead, they are dead!'

'Who are these people?'

Realising he had gaffed, Mitchell stuttered, 'North Koreans! Chinese! It was in the Korean War!'

'Who were your clients?' I reiterated, 'Sunday school teachers from St Ivel-in-the-Fridge?'

Sir R intervened, 'I am advising you, Mr Mitchell to say nothing.'

'I don't wish to impugn your professionalism, Sir Reginald, but are you used to criminal matters? You seem a bit out of your depth?' head cocked to one side, C-C intervened.

After much humming and hawing Sir R admitted that he was normally a real estate lawyer, and he was only representing Mitchell as a favour to Lord Lucas, as he was having difficulty finding a lawyer after gossip had made him *persona non grata* with much of the high echelon of London solicitors.

'Mr Mitchell, do you wish for Sir Reginald to continue to represent you, or do you wish to have a Legal Aid solicitor?'

Mitchell was a realist. He knew that Legal Aid solicitors tended to be the young and inexperienced, or the old and feeble, so he decided that any sort of posh lawyer was better than legal aid. And he needed to get his money's worth from that tight chinless wonder. 'I'd like to keep you, Sir Reginald,' he growled.

It took a bit more questioning before the oyster opened up and revealed the names of the Sheldons as hirers. 'They said a couple of nosy plods up North had been queering their pitch by busting a couple of runs across Morecambe Bay. They said that a couple of their people had disappeared without trace. They reckoned these two coppers had snuffed them ad buried the bodies under some new council houses. Was it you two?'

We bowed in unison and I said, 'Let me introduce myself and my colleague – voted Lancashire Executioners of the year! And of course we haven't killed anyone, but certain people who were troubled by being attached to the Sheldons have been rescued, and several London gangsters are now in jail. As will you be, Mr Mitchell!'

Sir R interrupted, 'Are you saying that you *are* executioners, Sergeant?'

'Don't be silly, Sir R,' C-C was scornful, 'if you want to mount a defence, you'll have to try much harder and more realistically than that. The whereabouts of the people that we rescued from London are known, and they all are safe and well, and their whereabouts documented and in the care of MI5 – so you categorically will not be allowed access to those documents.'

'Now, Sir Reginald, if we may continue, Mr Mitchell...' Under sustained but legal interrogation Mitchell told us he had been the sergeant major of Lord Lucas' regiment, 'And a right toffee-nosed, superior burk he was. But I was out of work, he knew my skill with a rifle, so suggested that I put the frighteners on you two.'

The frighteners? I doubted it.

C-C rushed out and had a conflab with Mr Forbes and the Superintendent. He came back quite a while later saying, 'The Inspector and the Superintendent have agreed that if you will give a full and honest statement, the charge will be reduced to Malicious Wounding.'

Smithy and I looked at each other gobsmacked. That was decidedly *not* legal. What were Forbsy and the Super up to?

'SO, Gentlemen,' started C-C, 'If the sergeants are agreeable, we will leave you to discuss with your lawyer what you wish to do.' And he hustled us out.

'Don't get your knickers in a knot, lads. Five and the Met are very close to tagging Mr Mitchell with several hits paid for by the Sheldons and a nasty Chinese dragon called Lee Ping. This way, he coughs his guts, and we hold him on this charge whilst we put together further charges – of murder!' Very sly, these sneaky-beakies.

When Lee learned that Mitchell had been arrested, he was incandescent. 'What sort of man you hire, Lucas?' his suave manner deserting him. 'Why you not hire decent hitman? Why can't you bribe these people you tell me are lowly police? Police always open to bribery. Why you not tell truth? *You* have money. *You* have drugs! You keep!' brushing aside Lucas' gabbled protestations, he continued, 'You very near to getting very close shave - from neck up. You choose – money or blood!'

Cutting off Lucas, he re-dialled. 'Sheldon? Which brother? Lucas tell me *you* have money; *you* have drugs!'

'That lying rat! We were robbed. The Filth arrested the trawler crew and seized the drugs and money. We sent a guy that Lucas reckoned was good to sort the cops. He got arrested – some snake must've shopped us. Wait till I find who it was!'

But Denise was long gone, spirited away by Virginia.

CHAPTER 29

The Sheldons were feeling ever more nervous. They no longer had any credibility at all in the East End, Lee was breathing threats and murder at them, and everywhere they went large men in raincoats and big boots followed them. Every time they went out in car a motor patrol stopped them on one excuse or another.

Lucas was feeling even more nervous. Other members of the aristocracy were shunning him. They accepted his criminality as little peccadillos as long as he was succeeding. But the faint smell of corruption – and even worse – failure was beginning to waft round him. His wife had gone on a protracted visit to her mother's, and in his club, the shunning continued. So he was grateful when Richard Sheldon rang.

'Listen, Yer Lordship, something very odd is going down with you and the Tong. I want a meet – tomorrow night – with you and Old Leaping. Cock and Bottle pub. Private room. 8.30. sharp!'

Lee felt Hong Kong breathing down his neck. He felt sure he was being swindled. No two mere PCs could do so much harm to a bunch of very feared gangsters – much less to his empire, so it must be Lucas or the Sheldons. And no one – absolutely *no one* robs the Triad. Heads will roll. He was in the middle of mobilising his soldiers to unleash his fury on Lucas and the Sheldons when the phone rang.

'Listen, Lee, you're on the wrong track here. We haven't robbed you, Lucas or anybody. Meet us and Lucas tomorrow night – Cock and Bottle pub. 8-30.'

Lee was offended. How dare an unschooled *Gaijin* talk to him like that! But he contained his anger. He could win this particular war, but the Sheldons weren't that softie Lucas. They could bite back and it was not in his interest to start a war. Here was a last chance to get his money without bloodshed.

Sister Virginia kept in touch with Amelia. She picked up quite a bit of what was going on in the street, snippets to pass on to me and Smithy. The 'ladies' were no longer scared of the Sheldons since most of their soldiers were known to be banged up; many were turning away to other pimps. Virginia and the other nuns were trying to get them to give up this life. The various stories of the nuns were enthralling, but what really reached the street culture was Sister Teresa, the ex-Circus Strong Woman. At first they couldn't believe a nun could have muscles, but after she'd arm-wrestled a few jack-the-lads around the pubs, and picked up the mouthiest and held him above her head, she was feted. And Virginia with her ex-professional background offered a listening ear and a waterproof shoulder for troubled males and females alike.

So it was that we got all the scuttlebutt from gangland – how a new team was coming in led by a huge Irishman called Cummins. How there were a lot of Chinese on the street – and a lot of plainclothes cops in bowlers and big boots.

It was how we learned of the tripartite meeting. Sister Virginia had the gossip and passed it on twelve hours before Special Branch saw fit to tell us. 'It's in a pub where we nuns are well known and welcome. I'll have a word with the landlord. He'll make sure we hear everything.'

'Don't you dare!' Smithy snapped, 'these guys are dangerous!'

'I'll be all right – I'll have Sister Teresa with me – no one will argue with her!'

I jumped in. 'Even Teresa can't ward off a bullet!'

'No but God can deflect it.' And with a sweet goodbye put the phone down.

'What a monster we've unleashed on the world! But isn't she the most agreeable and sweetest explosion you've ever come across!' Smithy grinned.

8.30 came. First came the Triad to case the joint. Then came the Sheldons. Finally Lucas, timidly, out of his depth among the rough dock workers. Each had two minders. Lee had large muscular minder and a skinny one. 'Watch the weedy-looking one, he's one of the top fighters in the country.' Richard whispered. The Sheldons' pair were two of his remaining enforcers, whilst Lucas brought two ex-soldiers from his former regiment, looking definitely outgunned amongst the real hard men. Virginia and Teresa were dressed in mufti as kitchen-skivvies. A very-nearly-closed serving hatch enabled the two nuns to hear every word.

The meeting started off icily polite. The Chinese cultural politeness and Lord Lucas' upbringing toned down the roughness of the Sheldons – for a while.

'I've told you what happened. Two consecutive shipments were intercepted by the police and the Royal navy, and the goods distrained.'

'You *told* us! Maybe true – maybe not.'

'how dare you, you...you...you *colonial!* I am an aristocrat – a man of honour!'

'Not too much honour to keep you away from whores and smuggling... *Your Lordship!*' sneered Lee. 'At least I am an honest gangster. Unlike these *Gaijin* gangsters, I have ethics.'

'You have ethics? Are you suggesting something?' hissed Rupert, the really dangerous brother. 'We lost out as well, more than you two fairies – we lost goods and men – and you expect us to pay for it?'

'*Your* gang, *your* boats – *your* responsibility! You pay – you too Lucas; your money or your life – isn't that what your highwaymen used to say? If you are telling the truth, you will die with a clear conscience,' Lee gave a macabre chuckle. The two soldiers looked decidedly nervy. This was not what they signed up for.

One of the Sheldon minders took out a flick knife and started ostentatiously to clean his fingernails with it. The skinny Chinese went and stood alongside him.

'I'm fed up to the back teeth with your lame excuses.' Tension bit. 'You tell me two thick rural plods run rings round you? If a lie – a pathetic one. If true - shame upon you – call yourselves gangsters!

'So! OK! Today you are in my company.it would be shameful to kill you here. But tomorrow you are fair game – no money has even been offered. So...suggest you make wills.'

It went quiet. Virginia and Teresa crept forward. The room was at boiling point. Lee glared at the Sheldons. The Sheldons sneered at Lee.

Lucas crept towards the door. The large Chinese and Sheldons' hoodlum moved to prevent it. Violence was in the air. A quiet muttering began, first a gentle hum. Then getting louder and louder, until the exchange of threats and epithets, English and Chinese, sounded like the clashing of Zulu shields before battle. Then, leaning too far, Virginia brought down a metal tray onto the serving hatch, opening it with a great crash.

The combatants turned towards the sound, blood in their eyes. With great presence of mind, Teresa took out a whistle kept from her PE lessons, blew hard and bellowed in a gruff masculine voice, 'Stop! Police! Stand where you are!'

The room emptied faster than an appeal at a charity dance. The grateful landlord rushed in. 'Drink, Sisters' pressing two large brandies on them.

The girls shook. 'That was close! We're teetotal, but for purely medicinal purposes...' they flopped onto a chair, trembling. The brandy went down then Virginia shook herself, stood and said, 'I must phone Bradkirk police at once.

We were off duty, but a cadet found us with C-C, Alicia and Amelia up at the hospital visiting Helen. 'Sarge! It's Sister! Here's the phone number. Wants you to phone immediately!' he gabbled.

Greyhound Smithy beat me to the hospital phone and was put through immediately. 'You alright?' he worried at her.

'We're OK but saved by the whistle!'

'Explain!' I demanded.

'We were hidden in the kitchen. The meeting degenerated, and was about to erupt. I leaned in too far, knocked over a tray and bashed the serving hatch open. There was a lot of violence in that room ready to engulf us. Teresa pulled out a games whistle from somewhere, gave an almighty blast and put on a big masculine voice.' She laughed shakily, 'You'd never believe how soft her normal speaking voice is, but she bellowed "Stop! Police!" They fled. But...' turning very quiet and serious, 'the Triad has taken a contract on both Sheldons and on Lucas. You must get them out of there!' Pronto!'

A quick explanation to the Two A's and Helen, and we were off back to the station. Forbesy was straight on to the Met, and C-C on to Five. Then we waited.

Lucas jumped into the Sheldons' car and gasped, 'Anywhere – we must talk!'

Mitchell settled in to prison life. It was not unlike the military – get up when told, do what you're told. Free food and uniform. Except he was back to squaddie and could no longer tell anyone what to do.

But when he had been there a couple of days, two huge prisoners, one black, one white came and walked either side of him. His pulse rate quickened and he looked round for a warder, but not a screw in sight.

'Gorra message for yer,' the white guy hissed.

'Yeh, a *serious* message growled the black guy, 'it's from your friends the Sheldons. This is it, "Tell Mr Mitchell he's a walking dead man. Tell him we don't like a failure and a grass"' He knew that the Sheldons regularly made people disappear under foundations, so he took it very seriously.

Mitchell was an excellent and decorated sniper, but he was not a scrapper. His expertise was hiding up a tree and killing at long range. He asked for an interview with the governor. The governor, a humane and kindly man - and a realist - offered time in Solitary Confinement until his appearing before the magistrates.

Smithy and I were called in as witnesses. The three magistrates were neither humane nor kindly. The chief magistrate was thin, acidulated and wore *pince-nez*. The other man was bluff and seemingly hearty, but in his mind was rather disappointed that flogging had been stopped. The lady was very superior; twin-set and genuine pearls and with an accent you could cut your fingers on.

The evidence was straight up-and-down. He was caught under a false name with a loaded 0.303 rifle with the serial number filed off, and – grave mistake, stupid for a professional – he had left his fingerprints on it. He was remanded into custody to Crown Court.

First, his defence asked for bail. Denied. Then asked, in view of the threat, to be remanded to a different prison. The lady sighed, 'Prisoners are always accusing others of threats,' she intoned haughtily. Bluff-and-hearty rather thought it would teach him a lesson if he were murdered. Acidulated the governor merely said, 'Refused.'

Mitchell panicked. Pushing the screw aside he leapt over the dock and ran down the aisle. Smithy took off after him like a hyperactive greyhound with me grampusing along in the rear. Mitchell sprinted down the street, pushing old ladies out of the way.

Until one brave old lass stuck her umbrella between her legs and began hitting him over the head with it, in best comic style. Smithy managed to calm her down and cuff Mitchell. I brought up the rear, and thanked the old lady profusely. Mitchell was swearing and sobbing as we took him back to the courtroom.

We rang the Super who came to the court and in his most stately fashion told the court that he took the threat seriously, that Mitchell was very much needed in a case involving national security, and that it was very important that he stay alive – at least at the moment. Therefore he asked the court to remand him to the custody of MI5.

Mitchell still faced the noose, but he was safe for the moment.

CHAPTER 30

Helen came out of hospital, though still in wheelchair. Amelia invited Smithy, Amelia, C-C and me. C-C, the sly dog, had been phoning and writing to Brenda Johnson and asked could he invite her. Amelia was overjoyed that Brenda was being supported after her husband's still-unsolved murder.

Lounging around after a belly-busting meal of steak egg and chips, we were talking idly.

'Smithy,' Amelia asked, 'have you always been a churchgoer?'

'No, I hated church. My parents were staunch and very boring Anglicans. So I had to go every week and listen to a pretentious old vicar. The only interesting bits I remember were the dreadful wickednesses us young people must beware of. Then I went to a minor public school that had regular boring church parades, more concerned about patriotism than God. I had the impression that if you didn't die in Egypt or Normandy you were a failure.'

'So what happened?'

'There was a girl in our village I rather fancied, but she was an ardent churchgoer, and said she couldn't go out with anyone not a Christian. So I started going,' intercepting a green eye from Alicia, 'Not nearly as gorgeous as you, Alicia!' he continued, ignoring a muttered *creep!* From Alicia. 'Anyway, I found a liveliness and a friendship there I never thought a church could produce – and after a few ifs and buts and maybes, gave my life over to Jesus – and have never regretted it.'

'What happened to the girl?'

'Nothing. She went off to Uni and I joined the police.'

Lucas and the Sheldon brothers holed up above a grotty inn in the East End. 'You say the Triad is after you?' asked Richard Sheldon, 'well, he's marked our card as well. He's blaming you and us for those shipments that went astray. We can't give him the money back so he wants our heads to show to Hong Kong. And he's a cruel bastard. It's as much about saving face as about the money.'

Breathing agitatedly, Lucas said, 'I have a plan. We must disappear. I have the use of a shooting lodge up in the Highlands of Scotland. I suggest we three, with a couple of helpers – and nobody else! – go up there and lie low. I don't think Lee will look up there. We can get some arms up there – the lodge is full of shotguns and rifles. Shooting is a major sport. There are always guns about, and nobody cares if you walk through the village carrying a shotgun – even in the off season. The lodge is quite away from the nearest road – any vehicle can be spotted a mile away. And if we are traced by Lee we'll need those guns!'

'Is that Smithy? Virginia here. A bit more scuttlebutt. The Sheldons have left home, and have booked into a cheap, rather grotty hotel in Whitechapel, the St Ivall's – not their usual style at all!'

'How do you get to know all this? Not that we're not grateful, you've done a lot for us.'

'The Guild of Prostitutes, Escorts and Allied Workers has an intelligence system that can knock MI5, MI6, CIA and KGB into a cocked hat. Then the lasses talk to me as I have coffee and chat with them. The word on the street seems to think the Sheldons are a spent force, and likely to be moving.'

'Thanks, Virginia, give your sisters our regards – especially the redoubtable Sister Teresa.'

'All part of the service, Gentlemen.'

Putting the phone down Smithy turned to me, 'We need Forbesy and the Super in on this – get the Met covering the Sheldons.'

After several fruitless phone calls, Forbesy turned to us, frowning, 'Sorry, lads, their Almightinesses at New Scotland Yard are too busy dancing around with Notting Hill race riots and CND marches to bother about a mere pair of major gangsters on their patch. So I've twisted their arms to let you two go and suss out what they're up to.'

We booked in to the St Iris's cheapest rooms as two down-on-their-luck labourers come to the Smoke from Newcastle. Then we selected suitable outfits. Smithy chose a pair of bogtrotting corduroy trousers several sizes too big with braces. He had an old army collarless shirt, an army sweater and a donkey jacket. I grabbed a pair of very faded cheap denims, an undervest and an ex-US Army parka. We both had tackety boots with string laces. Smithy dyed his blond hair black. I just let mine blow. We thought Smithy's hands were too dishwasher-soft so he wore bandages – caustic soda burns from his last job.

And there we sat bored for two weeks. We saw the Sheldons and – surprisingly – Lucas dressed like a dosser. Discreetly following we saw them pick up hiking gear, rucksacks and the new Vibram-soled boots. Nostrils flaring with the stink of fish we phoned C-C. He reported that Lucas had a part ownership of a shooting lodge in the highlands.

Came the day, first a Sheldon crept out at 5a.m. then Lucas. Then another Sheldon. The streets too empty to follow them we took a chance and a taxi to King's Cross. Sure enough, they arrived singly and got on the next train north. Getting in another carriage, we lay low. At Edinburgh they caught a train to Aviemore. We quickly bought hiking gear and followed on the next train.

Arriving at Aviemore – a real frontier town straight from Hollywood, we sought the local bobby who told us 'His Lorrdsheep and friends had taken a shooting lodge – the Macamaclashan Lodge near Ultwullie.' We let Forbesy and C-C know then booked into the Youth Hostel.

CHAPTER 31

Grannie Sheldon hobbled to the door to answer a loud knocking.

'Who is it?'

'Hoo Lee Wang. I am dilector of Hong Kong finest silk merchants. Have bizniz with Mistahs Sherdon!' Intoned Lee Wang in his best music hall Chinese accent.

As Grannie opened it, she was pushed violently over, and six burly Chinamen rushed in, followed by smoothy Chinese person. She was picked up and thrust down onto a chair. Her arms and legs were roughly tied, then the smoothy spoke, raising his pork pie hat. 'Excuse my colleagues, madam, they are not used to handling ladies. All we need to know is where your grandsons are. They have something of mine.'

The vituperation that followed would make a London docker blush.

'Oh, that's not very ladylike – Mr Ma, please gag her. Now all we want to know – I repeat – is where your grandsons are.' Gurglings behind the gag. 'Loose her, Mr Ma.'

'I ain't tellin' yer nothin'!'

'Oh, I think you will. Mr Chou, go and find a pillow case and soak it.'

Brutally grabbing the old lady's hair, he pulled her head back. Chou slapped the sopping pillowcase over her face and held it tight. She couldn't scream. She couldn't breathe. Her arms and legs spasmed against their bonds.

'Release her! Now, dear lady, where have your grandsons gone?'

More vituperation. More pillowcase. Finally she cracked. This horrible old bat who had laughed gleefully when she saw Richard and Rupert tortured someone was a breathless, sobbing wretch. 'It's Scotland! They're guests of a lord!' *Lucas!* Thought Lee. *We'll kill three birds with one stone!*

'Now, Mr Dee, a drink of water for the lady.' And holding her head back he poured the water into her mouth – more and more. It ran out of her nose. She took a shuddering breath and her heart stopped.

'Right, Gentlemen, off to Scotland we go!' raking the burning coals from the fireplace onto the hearth rug, and laughing gleefully as it blazed.

Angus McAngus welcomed the three. 'Ye'll no be wantin' shootin'. Too earrly in the year!'

'No, That's fine, Angus, my business colleagues and I just need a rest – and some of your wife's famous Scotch pies. We have had a very busy time and we need a break. We may take some shotguns after rabbits.

'Also can you do me a favour? Several of our other colleagues want us to sign a deal with Hong Kong. And we are exhausted. Can you let us know if any Asiatic gentlemen come looking for us?'

C-C pulled some strings with the G.O.C. Scotland in Edinburgh Castle and brought a sergeant and six stocky, competent-looking and fully-armed Argylls up with him. We got the local cops to keep a distant eye on the shooting lodge but *do not approach.* We warned them how dangerous and how tense these guys were. 'They're like sweating gelignite. One smell of a cop car could result in mayhem.

After a while the three appeared in the local pub, not very popular with the locals as they overtly despised them, Lucas looking down his nose at the hoi polloi and the Sheldons raucously and unfavourably comparing the local people with Londoners. Nonetheless the innate politeness and hospitality of the Highlanders saved them a working over by large muscular forest workers.

Smithy pushed his luck. He dressed himself in a shrieking yellow tartan kilt and a green sweater. He assumed a red wig and tucked a skian dhu down a pair of ordinary socks. Then he practised a Canadian accent. Bounding into the bar, he announced himself, 'Hi, I'm Peter! My ma came from Scotland so I thought I'd visit! Pints for everybody!' I cringed as I lurked in the background in my down-on-my-luck outfit. Smithy went round everybody shaking hands. He shook hands with Lucas, 'Say! A real lord? Ermine and all that?'

Lucas smiled a superior smile and said, 'Yes, old boy. Normally I come up here for the shooting.'

'Shooting peasants?' carolled Smithy, chortling at his own joke. His Lordship smiled a wintry superior smile.

Smithy sat down with the gang and chattered like a long Canadian monkey. Asking Lucas what it was like to be part of such an old-established way of life, 'It must be very special to you, do you have a big house? Is London a good place to live – the capital of the British Empire? I've had a quick visit and the place seemed full of foreigners, Indians, Pakistanis, Negroes – but especially Chinese. Is it like that all the time or is the hub of Empire the place to visit? How do you all find it? And you guys? What's it like being His Lordship's servants? "What ho, Jeeves," and all that?' The Sheldons, highly offended just growled and muttered. I reached for my short truncheon, fearing mayhem. But Smithy rose and carried on his merry way. I sweated. The guy has a death wish.

'You staying long, Sir?' inquired the landlord, 'do you need a room?'

'Heck, no, just called in, I'm on the next train to In-veer-ness! Staying with Cousin Archie – he's a real Scot!' then he swanned out of the door.

Back in the boarding house, he gleefully related his bit of drama to C-C and the soldiers. C-C cringed. The sergeant growled, 'ye'll get yer heid kicked in ye daft buggerrr!'

'What was all the play-acting, Smithy?' C-C enquired, 'you didn't learn anything!'

'Of course I did. I learned that they are all carrying. They all had a suspicious bulge under their jackets. So they are prepared – and ready! – to shoot. I also learned that they're very nervous. The way they were talking loudly about haggis-bashers and thick peasants; trying to give themselves the authority in this to them backward place that they once had in the Smoke. Kidding themselves they are still in charge. Hiding the scars.'

'Scum like ye tell us they are dinna have scars,' growled the youngest Argyll.

''Afraid they do, lad,' said Smithy quietly, 'His Lordship, having all the rank and privilege of an aristocracy that's a hangover from a bunch of Norman invaders – he will be deeply offended at such cavalier treatment by the Lower Orders. And the Sheldons, they had the rank and privilege of being the Gang of Gangs in the underbelly of the Capital. Lucas is a peer; the Sheldons were kings, feared by all for their psychopathy. But we have robbed them of it – Lucas' friends no longer speak to him – he daren't even appear in the House of Lords and his marriage is on the rocks. And he's broke. Special Branch and a Tong are also putting pressure on him

'And the Sheldons? Their people keep disappearing or getting banged up, they no longer get fear and respect, and their grubby empire is crumbling. And MI5 and Lee Ping are on their case as well. They are feeling hunted. And my silly bit of nonsense brought out all their angst and desperation. And Bill, did you notice they all kept glancing at the door, and tensed every time someone came in? We can begin to exert pressure on them. I also overheard that the remnants of the Sheldon gang are on their way up, six hard cases.'

'What can we do, Sirrs?' asked the sergeant in his soft Western Isles burr, his eyes lighting up at the promise of action.

'A couple of things, gents,' said C-C, 'Very subtly appear in twos or threes in the, pub. Keep not-so-noticeably glancing over at the gangsters. Keep walking past the shooting lodge. I've brought some cameras. Shoot the wildlife and countryside all round their lodge, getting the house in every time. That should spook them. But stay alert and be armed. These guys are killers but without your army discipline and ethics. Treat this like Aden or Malaya. It could get that rough.'

'Aye, we can do that – I was a stalker before I joined, and we've all seen action in Malaysia, Aden and Kenya.'

'OK, and thanks, lads. And Bill and Smithy, you stay out of it. Remember you were targets not long ago – and probably still are.'

CHAPTER 32

Lee called together his finest and most brutal soldiers, and gave strict instructions. 'We are no longer enforcing – we are going to kill. If we let these *Gaijin* scum get away without paying our share of the failed deliveries, and don't deliver heads on a platter, then Hong Kong will want *our* heads on a platter. We will hire a minibus to travel up, that way we can carry our arsenal with us. So get a shotgun and a 0.38 each with much ammunition. Wong Ha and Hang Sao, draw a No4T sniper rifle each. And, all of you - don't worry about civilian casualties, the Scots are even more uncouth than the English!

'And I have booked us hotels in pairs in Inverness – we don't want to fill Aviemore with Chinese faces – until the time is right. I and Jeng Bao will stay quite openly in the Grampian Hotel in Aviemore and we will plan out our attack.'

The days passed uneventfully, the Jocks kept a close watch on Lucas and co, I read Jack London, Smithy read his Bible and prayed – and every night spent ages phoning Alicia.

Then Iain, the most innocuous-looking Argyll noticed two Chinese-looking gentlemen – lee Ping with one of his team, no doubt - disguised as tourists. They took bus excursions every day, but our lads happened to see them casing the shooting lodge where Lucas and co were. They also reported another six cockneys had arrived and were staying in the lodge. Things were building up.

C-C growled quietly, 'we must get the tong and Lucas and the Sheldons out of the town; neither group are bothered about killing anyone in the way. If there's a bloodbath – let it be out in the country. And let it be them! And we have to get Angus out of there, the local cops rate him as an honest man – apart from a bit of poaching. He just looks after the house for the syndicate. We don't want any bits of lead flying his way.'

Smithy's ears pricked up. 'A syndicate? A little pressure on them would maybe get Lucas and the thugs moving. Get them in the open and arrest them without bloodshed.'

C-C was phoning the mother-ship before you could say spook. We heard lots of 'Uhuh! 'OK, Sure Thing's and finally C-C put the phone down. 'Well, you guys, the syndicate is owned by six men, two of them MPs, another lord and two rich business owners -all posh and jealous of their privileges – and very easily spooked. And my boss is right now on the phone to all of them, putting in the bubble about Lucas. I reckon he'll be out of there before you could say 'embarrassment.'

'But we'd better keep an eye on Lee Ping,' I mused. 'He won't be up here for a healthy skiing holiday.'

'I also got permission to put a tap on his phone so we will know where he is going,' said C-C.

Lee Ping drove up to Inverness for a council of war. 'By a little subtle questioning from the Head Director of Hoo Lee Wang, importer of fine Chinese silks, we now know where both Lucas and the gangsters are staying. They are holed up near a little village near Aviemore. They are very fearful, and trying to prove themselves by being rude to the local people. We'll let themselves get a bit more worked up – then we strike!'

'Who's this head Director?' enquired Jao Ling, the strongest but the thickest of the Tong squad. Hang Sao cuffed him round the ear, 'Who do you think, Dummy?'

'Ohh…yeah!'

'And…' continued Lee imperturbably, 'I have put a phone tap on Lucas' phone.' He preened, 'as these colonising English say, "Deuced cunning, these Chinese." So we will know all the time what they are up to. Then we pounce. Then we kill them, pickle their heads and dispatch them to Hong Kong.'

The gang smiled in anticipation.

Smithy and I walked up to the lodge when Lucas and co were down in the pub, 'Mr McAngus, we need a quiet word,' showing our warrant cards, 'You and Mrs McAngus are in grave danger. We can't go into details, but there is a matter of national security. Please both pack quickly. The Government is moving you some where quiet in England until the problem is resolved.'

'Och I didna like His Lorrdship's sairvants. They look a rough bunch – an' Sassenach cityites. But His lordship is always a good tipper – if ye know yer place. And they all treat me like ah'm mentally defective. Ah'll no be sorry for a wee holiday on the govairnment. If it's really that bad.'

'It is! We wouldn't go to all this trouble otherwise. You *must* go – as soon as you've packed.

Lucas drove back to the Lodge, although he had tried every available single malt. The Sheldons and their thugs were cock-a-hoop, having nearly got into a fight with local foresters, a proud lot getting impatient with them and wanting to avenge Culloden, by singing scurrilous songs about Scottish girls and what Scots have under their kilts. They were saved a pasting by the local bobby.

'You don't want to pick a fight wi' that lot,' the bobby told them, 'These guys have muscles in places normal people don't even have places. You may be hard cases where you come from, but these guys will play football with your heid, using your arm and legs for goalposts.'

Full of bagpipe broth and vainglory they sang all the way home.

'McAngus! McAngus! Where the devil are you?' bellowed a drunken Lordship, 'Where are you? I need you! Food! Drink! And you've let the fire go out!' but answer came there none. He sobered up enough to go to bed, grumbling all the way.

10.30 net morning the insistent clangour of the phone bell dragged him into sick-feeling, headachy and semi-consciousness.

'Is that lord Lucas?' inquired a genteel female voice, 'hold the line please I have the Honourable Richard Trescothick, MP on the telephone for you.' Head pounding, Lucas groaned into the phone, 'Hello, Dickie. How nice to hear you.'

'Lucas, my friend, what have you been up to?'

'How do you mean, Dickie?'

'All the rest of our little shooting-party have had the spooks from MI5 interrogating – *interrogating!* us about you. You are very *persona non grata* with the security services so you are now *persona non grata* with us!'

'What can you mean?'

'You are no longer part of our syndicate. So you no longer have any right to use the Lodge. We want you out by Saturday.' Two separate bunches of phone-tapping sneaky-beakies grinned.

There followed frantic phone calls; Lucas trying to find alternative accommodation.

'They've got a couple of cottages booked just the other side of Aviemore itself down the A9. I got the address, chief.'

C-C called us together. 'We know where they're moving and when they're moving. So can we have you Jocks in uniform and armed and we'll stage an ambush. There's some thick forest on both side of the road near a village called Kincraig, just before Aviemore. We'll get them there.'

Lee called the Tong together. 'We know where they're moving and when they're moving. We'll follow them down the A9 until we reach some woods near a one-hole place called Kincraig. Then we'll ram them and execute them.'

CHAPTER 33

Saturday brought tension. Tension in the Lodge with Lucas and the Sheldon crew. Lucas had enquired about McAngus. No one had heard a thing. He just disappeared. Lucas began to feel paranoid. 'He must be somewhere, the leprechauns can't have taken him!'

'Leprechauns are Irish, Chief.'

'Don't lecture me, you uncouth wretch! And don't call me chief!'

'Roighty-ho, yer lordship,' intoned Richard, tugging his forelock.

Lucas snarled but said no more. He may need their guns.

Tension was rife among the Tong. Dragged away from Inverness to steal a lorry, they managed to steal a Bedford three-tonner. Under his inscrutable demeanor, Lee was a bag of nerves. If Lucas' head and the Sheldons' heads didn't roll, his surely would. And he didn't make a comfortable boss when he was like this. The tong soldiers crept around, scared to attract his attention. Little Lou, thankfully out of Lee's wrath, kept an eye on the Lodge from a garden shed in the grounds.

We parked up near the woods. Five of the Argylls changed into uniform, Smithy and I donned grey anoraks and big boots, and C-C stayed his usual Saville Row self. Iain, the innocuous-looking Argyll stayed in civvies; donkey jacket and overalls, and took a Post Office tent, a Post Office BSA Bantam motorcycle, a sidearm and a walkie-talkie and staked out the Lodge.

Hours passed. There was coming and going round the lodge as the gangsters loaded the cars and loaded their guns. We crouched in the trees like coiled springs, the banter died and we sat like twitchy Buddhas in need of Trilafon. We checked our arms; 0.303s for the soldiers, 0.38" Colts for me and C-C. and of course Smithy with his faithful nunchuka.

The Sheldons' cars moved. Little Lou sprinted down the road to where Lee's vehicle was parked and leapt aboard.

Smithy's walkie-talkie crackled into life. 'It's go! Down the A9 towards Perth! I'm on the bike and moving!' we quickly blocked the road with a tractor and trailer, and took up firing-positions. The lead car barrelled round the corner and hit the trailer. The other two cars screeched to a halt.

But then a Bedford three-ton lorry charged round the bend and smacked into the third car. Chinese gangsters boiled out. The gangsters split and ran into the woods followed by the Triad. C-C waved the troops after them. The soldiers, jungle trained, ghosted after the combatants. Ill-dressed and ill-equipped for forest warfare the Triad and the Sheldons could be seen firing at every shadow and crashing through the trees. There was a scream as a Chinese body flopped with a bullet in the chest. Then a sigh as a gangster slowly fell down – dead.

The Argylls moved like khaki ghosts towards the fight. A Tong warrior fell over a tree root and was pounced on, gagged and handcuffed. Richard Sheldon, the suave urbanite, fell, shot dead in a puddle. Rupert went berserk, charging an Argyll, screaming. A single round, and he died still screaming. The noise died down as the combatants died. Finally, the two remaining gangsters and the single tongster surrendered and were quickly secured. But of Lucas or Lee Ping there was not a trace.

There was the putter of a two-stroke engine and a crash as Iain joined in, leaping off the bike and shooting an escaping gangster dead.

Silence fell over the forest as we gathered up the dead and arrested.

We moved the trailer to let in the ambulances and the paddy wagons. The Argylls lined up on parade. Not a scratch on any of them. The sergeant marched up to us, saluted and barked, 'troops ready for inspection, Sirs!' We recognised what an honour that was, and shook hands with everyone and congratulated them on an awesomely fine and efficient job. They beamed with pride.

Two weeks later, midnight, a ragged Chinese gentleman and an equally ragged Peer of the Realm, united by misfortune, were sailing a small puttering motorboat wearily towards France. They were too exhausted to notice the silent, lightless approach of a cabin-cruiser. Dark shapes silently boarded and efficiently cut two throats, throwing the headless bodies overboard and leaving the little boat to circle aimlessly until the fuel ran out. The cabin cruiser silently purred away with the heads in ice packs.

CHAPTER 34

Time passed. Smithy and I were recommended for the Police Gallantry Awards – and had to go to London to receive them. A lot of fuss.

Smithy and I were also recommended to the Home Office by C-C's bosses at MI5 to be accepted into a very clandestine bunch of police counter-terrorism sneaky-beakies disguised as a university sociology department operating from an office near Euston station. There was plenty to keep us going down there. The KGB and MKVD were both trying to outdo each other in Britain, double agents were crawling out of the woodwork, disaffected left-wing students and right-wing no-hopers were getting a bit frisky and kicking off about Black and Asian immigrants. There were amazingly, still a few Nazis creeping round, saying Hitler wasn't dead. But the vast bulk of the population settled down to never having it so good, doing football pools and being teddy-boys.

Once we were settled, Smnithy and Alicia were married up in Bradkirk. I was Best Man, and Amelia and a still-hobbling Helen were Matron of Honour and bridesmaid. Forbesy, the Super and their wives were there, Fred Thompson made a grand job of giving Alicia away, and C-C – now more or less permanently with Brenda Johnson cheered them from the sidelines.

Smithy continued to study Judo, Eastern European languages and cryptography. I did a B Sc in criminology and sociology, and we settled down to try to out-think the KGB, red terrorists and Nazi terrorists. Smithy and Alicia found a church near them, and Alicia made ward-sister, then had a daughter, and we were fine.

The end...For a while...

FIFTYSPEAK

Plod	An English policeman
The Filth;	the Old Bill Police
Screw	A prison warder
Scotch pies	Delicious mutton confectionary
Barm cake	a bread roll; also someone a bit dopey
The Goon Show	A famous iconoclastic radio comedy
Glasshouse	Military prison
Cough	Information given by an informant.
Trilafon	A sedative popular with GP's in the 50s

THE AUTHOR

Bill Watson is the pen-name of Rev. Jim Crompton; a church minister ordained in both the Baptist Church and the Congregational Church – 'I never seem to do anything by halves' he claims.

Jim was born in Lancashire in 1943, and went to his local grammar school and hated it. 'The only thing my headmaster and I ever agreed on was that I should leave as soon as possible,' he claims. He racketed around doing many jobs; metallurgic technician, oil technician, farm labourer, warehouse man, delivery driver, baker, four years in the RAF as a Russian Linguist and for many years a teacher of Special Needs students.

He became a Christian while in Teacher Training College, and was ordained four years later, serving in needy areas.

When not scribbling, Jim likes to walk, sort out a garden, and enjoy an occasional wild swim off the highest beach in Britain – Loch Morlich.

Jim shares his life with one wife of forty-five years, two children, two children-in-law, nine grandchildren and four dopey hens.

Lightning Source UK Ltd.
Milton Keynes UK
UKHW042240011122
411404UK00015B/145